SEEKING REDEMPTION

ELIZABETH JOHNS

For Tina. This one would not have happened without you.

CHAPTER 1

LONDON, 1808

*L*ady Lydia Markham watched Lord Fairmont from the corner of her eye. She always knew where he was, she could not help it. He was magnificent. He stood a head taller than the crowd, his golden hair and grey eyes captivating her. She was drawn to him like a magnet, unable to resist the pull of his opposite force drawing her to him. She shook her head. She had to stop thinking such things. For one, Lord Fairmont would never give her a second glance. For two, her aunt had warned her that bluestockings were not desirable marriage material. Books had been her only companion for the last several years. If that made her a bluestocking, her aunt had no one to blame but herself.

She had scarce social experience, having been brought up by a childless aunt and uncle who did not have time for her. When her parents died, she had been deposited in the country with her nurse. And, as if suddenly remembered by her aunt, she found herself thrust into a London Season, barely aged nineteen. She was trying her best to fit into this vastly new world, *the beau monde*. Her uncle was a prominent political voice in Parliament, and she was the well-dowered daughter of an earl. She was expected to make a brilliant match this season.

"Lydia, dearest," her aunt spoke.

Lydia reluctantly pulled her eyes away from Lord Fairmont.

"Yes, Aunt?"

"I would like to introduce you to the Duchess of Loring and her niece, Miss Sarah Abbott. She is newly out this Season as well and would be a beneficial acquaintance."

"I would be pleased to meet her." And she would. A friend would be most welcome in this daunting experience. They waited until the Duchess and Miss Abbott were not engaged before approaching.

"Good evening, Yvonne, is this your new protégé?" The Duchess addressed her aunt as a casual friend.

"Yes, may I present Lady Lydia Markham? Lydia, this is her Grace, the Duchess of Loring, and her niece Sarah, Miss Abbott."

Lydia made her curtsies and was drawn aside by Miss Abbott.

"How is it that I have never heard of you before?" Miss Abbott asked boldly, apparently trying to determine if she was friend or foe.

"I am uncertain. I have lived in the country, at my aunt and uncle's home, for several years."

"Your aunt has never mentioned you, however," Miss Abbott said in consternation.

"I do not believe she gives me a second thought when I am not in her presence," Lydia said with brutal honesty.

Miss Abbott seemed to mull this information over. She must have decided in Lydia's favour, for she took her arm as if they were old acquaintances.

"Do you have your eye on anyone in particular?"

"No." She shook her head. She was not brave enough to admit her fascination for Lord Fairmont to a new acquaintance, anyway. No matter his was the only name and face she knew from her time in London thus far. Why else would she bother when she had found perfection? If he would only look at her. Just once.

"And yourself?"

Miss Abbott waved her hand. "I am already betrothed. Our fathers arranged the match."

"Oh, dear. I am sorry." Lydia thought that sounded terrible.

"I am not. Have you seen him?" Miss Abbott scanned the room and indicated behind her. "He is standing next to my brother and cousin over there."

Lydia squeezed her eyes and said a quick prayer. Please don't let it be Lord Fairmont. She turned and opened her eyes. Of course, Lord Fairmont was standing exactly where Miss Abbott had indicated. She must have gasped out loud.

"He is divine, is he not? Come, I shall introduce you. Beware of my cousin, however. He is quite the rake. My aunt says he will grow out of this phase, but he is currently sowing fields and fields of wild oats." Miss Abbott laughed.

Where did all the farming analogies come from, Lydia wondered? She had no choice but to follow. She would prefer to wallow in misery, but she smiled and braced herself to finally meet the man of her dreams. Who was betrothed to someone else.

"Good evening, gentlemen. May I present Lady Lydia Markham? Lady Lydia, my betrothed, Lord Abernathy, my brother, Lieutenant Andrew Abbott and my cousin, Lord Fairmont."

Had she said cousin?

Lord Abernathy took her hand first and brushed a kiss across her fingertips. "It is a pleasure to meet you, Lady Lydia."

"And you, my lord." She proffered a curtsy. Then Lieutenant Abbott greeted her likewise.

She turned to meet the man she had dreamt of for weeks. And met his cravat. It was a lovely, crisply starched and mathematically tied cravat. She finally looked up and locked eyes with him. She was lost in grey seas. Knowing crinkles formed around his twinkling eyes. She had to bite her lower lip to prevent her jaw from gaping open.

"Lady Lydia." He took her hand in his, placed a purposeful kiss and continued to hold it. Her name had never sounded so lyrical. "Charmed."

She heard a drumming in her ears. Was that her knees knocking so loudly?

"Is this dance already spoken for?" his musical voice asked.

3

She felt a subtle nudge from Miss Abbott. "No, no, my lord. I would be pleased to dance with you."

$\sim$

Nathaniel, Lord Fairmont, and heir to the Duke of Loring, was bored. Another ball with insipid débutantes. He had just escaped another lecture from his parents on ceasing his dissipation, settling down, doing his duty, etcetera, etcetera. Had his father ever actually looked at the crowds of débutantes? Besides, he had loads of time. He was barely four-and-twenty. He had no intention of putting on leg shackles until absolutely necessary.

Why would he knowingly sign up for constant lectures on reforming himself when his parents performed that task admirably? Bachelorhood was entirely too pleasurable. He and his closest friends entertained themselves nightly with extravagant diversions. Well, he certainly entertained himself nightly. His friends could not handle their whisky like he could. He was itching for the moment when he would have done his duty at this ball and could leave and seek out his mistress, instead of wiping the dribble from the faces of these infants. Unless...

"Andrew, who is that delicious specimen standing next to your sister?"

"No idea. But fret not, it looks as if we shall soon find out."

Nathaniel watched a brunette beauty with porcelain skin float towards him on his cousin's arm. She must have been hidden away on another continent, for she would never have escaped his notice otherwise. She did not look like a débutante, even though she was dressed as one. Perhaps he could do his duty a little longer than usual tonight.

He watched as she approached and their eyes met briefly. Lady Lydia was her name. He liked the sound rolling off his tongue. He could say that all night. Apparently she liked the way it sounded too, for she blushed from head downward when he said it. The evening suddenly held promise.

He took the beauty in his arms for a dance.

"So, Lady Lydia…" He lingered on each L. "…Tell me how you have escaped my notice before now?"

He expected her to blush again, but she held her composure—even more promising.

"I am not certain, my lord. I suspect having been in Wiltshire these past several years might be the reason." She looked him straight in the eye.

"I must make a note to visit Wiltshire soon if this is what she produces."

She laughed, "I was not *produced* in Wiltshire, as you so eloquently put it. I would hate for you to be disappointed. What a strange conversation this is!"

"I see you are not used to the art of flirtation." He regarded her with amusement.

"No, sir," she said demurely. "You will be disappointed in me if that is your expectation."

"*Au contraire.* You are performing admirably. And I will be most happy to instruct you in any way, should I find you lacking." His eyes sparkled with meaning.

"You are most gracious, my lord," she said with a hint of sarcasm. She might be a débutante, but she had some mettle.

"Now, back to where you were produced. I must know." He was actually interested, for once.

"France, my lord. My mother was French, and I spent my childhood there. I was sent to Wiltshire when my parents died. My uncle Dannon is my guardian."

"So he is married to your maternal aunt? Your father was English?" She nodded.

"You have not been long in London. I can see you will need some tutoring. May I begin by offering to drive you in the park tomorrow afternoon?" He held his arm out to escort her.

"I would enjoy that, thank you." She smiled genuinely, not in a practised manner, and he was hooked.

"Tut, tut. Lesson number one, you must ask your aunt's permission before accepting. You never know, I might be a heartless rake whom you should avoid." She could not say she was not warned, at least.

"I doubt my aunt would care overly much. Your cousin already informed me that you are a rake and sowing your wild oats," she said with refreshing frankness.

He laughed and led her off the floor toward the refreshment table.

"One can only conclude, however, that you do not know the definition of those terms."

"Perhaps not, but it will be your duty as my tutor to instruct me."

She need not ask twice, heaven help him. "I would be delighted." She had no idea.

CHAPTER 2

*L*ydia was in love. She didn't know what had hit her. Lord
Fairmont had swept her off her feet, and he seemed to recip-
rocate her feelings. He had eyes only for her, according to her
aunt. She was taken on daily rides and was danced with every night.
Fresh flowers arrived every day, and envious eyes followed her every
move. The ton was amazed. Even his parents seemed delighted.

"Of course my aunt and uncle are delighted," Miss Abbott had said.
"They see you as his saviour from his profligate lifestyle."

Lydia could not believe his reputation was true. She had not seen
that side of Lord Fairmont. He never overindulged in her presence,
and if he had a mistress, he never spoke of her. Her aunt said that was
to be expected, and Lydia was not supposed to know of such things. A
lady looked the other way. Lydia did not know about that, but she was
certain once they were married he would settle down.

Tonight there was to be a masquerade ball at Lord Eversham's. It
was not considered a proper place for débutantes, but she would be in
costume. Who would know? Miss Abbott was attending with her
grandmama, so how improper could it be? She knew Lord Fairmont
would be there and she wanted to be near him every chance she could.
She did not know if her aunt would tolerate her presence another

Season if she did not bring Lord Fairmont up to scratch, as she'd heard it vulgarly phrased.

When she'd told her aunt she was spending the evening with Miss Abbott, she had not even been asked any questions.

Miss Abbott had sent over a costume for her to wear. It was supposed to be Aphrodite. She certainly did not feel like she had more on than the statue. Thank God she would be wearing a mask. She could only hope to keep Lord Fairmont all to herself tonight and convince him that he need look no more. He had dropped several hints about their future, but had never uttered the phrase, *Will you marry me?*

She was not quite ready when Miss Abbott arrived.

"Please show her up," she told her maid when informed of her visitor.

"Very good, my lady."

When Miss Abbott saw her she gasped. "Oh Lydia! I had no idea...I asked the Madame to send over a costume...but goodness me!"

"Should I not go? I confess I feel rather naked!" she asked worriedly.

"My cousin will not be able to take his eyes off you, that is certain! Make sure you never remove the mask!" Miss Abbott walked around her. Naked was not precisely accurate, for there was a good deal of fabric draped over her, but it was a thin white material that left little to the imagination and her upper back exposed.

Lydia looked at Miss Abbott's demure Bo Peep costume and wanted to faint.

"I suppose it is too late to change now." She was disappointed. She did not want to stay at home.

"It will be all right, but keep your cloak on until my grandmother is safely ensconced in the card room," Miss Abbott warned.

Nathaniel could not believe how he felt about Lady Lydia. He could actually foresee settling down with her one day—but not yet. He could certainly wait a while longer. He was not ready to give up his bachelorhood when that meant giving up his other pleasures. But he would, when the time was right. Many people were betrothed for years. His own sister was betrothed to Lord Vernon and she was not even out of the schoolroom yet. Perhaps he would speak with Lydia's uncle on the morrow. For tonight, he would enjoy the masquerade. It was a shame Lydia was a débutante, or he would have enjoyed her presence there. But he was not married yet. He shrugged and downed another dram of whisky, followed by a draw on a pipe.

The whisky choked in his throat when he saw Aphrodite walk in. Vernon slapped him on the back and he swore under his breath. He set his pipe and drink down to catch his breath.

"Nathaniel is finally moonstruck. I shall enjoy watching him fall into the parson's mousetrap, and make a cake of himself while doing it!" his cousin Andrew mused.

Nathaniel did not hear a word Andrew said.

"Better get to her first, old chap. The vultures are beginning to circle," Vernon warned.

He immediately made his way to her side, along with every other unoccupied male in the room. He reached her first.

"Oh, goddess of beauty," he addressed her and proffered a gallant bow, "may I have this dance?"

He pulled her into his arms before she could answer. He looked down. Could she be more beautiful?

"What are you doing here, Lydia?" he whispered in her ear. She shivered.

"How did you know?" she asked anxiously.

"How would I not know you?"

"Is it so obvious? Perhaps I should leave."

"Only to me." By gads, she looked and felt glorious. He should take her home. She could not expect a hot-blooded male to keep his hands off her, dressed as she was, at a party like this. The room was teeming with lions on the hunt.

"I am sorry if I should not be here. Are you angry? I only wanted to be with you," she said disappointedly.

"No. Angry is not the word I would choose. Vexed, perhaps. I do believe you are too naïve for your own good. Or mine." He wanted her there, but did not necessarily want every other man to see this much of his future wife. He pulled her closer. He would not have expected this of her. He smiled. Perhaps being married to her would be more adventurous than he thought. He pulled at his collar. It was getting hot in there. He needed to cool down, and quickly. He wish he had not drunk so much before. It was hard enough thinking clearly around her when he was sober.

"Shall we take a walk outside? I am becoming overheated in this crush."

"Of course."

He led her out to the terrace and along the paths to a more secluded spot where they could speak in private. The moonlit night and the fragrant smell of the garden were euphoric to the senses. He led her to a bench. Perhaps this was not such a brilliant idea either. She snuggled up next to him and he had to take a deep breath. She shivered again.

"Are you cold?" He had not considered she was not wearing much clothing. That was his reason for being hot. He put his arms around her to keep her warm. He was doing his best to be a gentleman, until she looked up at him with those big eyes. They sparkled in the moonlight, and before he realized he was lost, he leaned down and kissed her.

Lydia had been warned about going into the garden alone. If this was what happened here, then she was sure the old biddies were just playing tricks on the débutantes. She felt magical. When Nathaniel kissed her, her insides caught on fire. The feeling was indescribable. She could not think straight. When his hands wondered to places she was certain were improper, she started to object until he reassured her.

"Nathaniel? Should we be doing this?"

"Just a glimpse of what it will be like when we are married," he muttered between kisses, reassuring her.

She was sure she had heard the word married. She wanted to give herself over completely, but something in the back of her mind would not let her fully enjoy herself if things got out of hand. She whispered his name in faint protest.

"Shh, my love. I'm only loving you."

Before she knew what was happening, he was on top of her and she lost all sense, intoxicated by him. It was too late before she realized what had happened.

"Lydia, I did not mean to let it go…"

She nodded into his chest. She felt happy and sad at the same time. As if sensing her confusion, he held her in his arms until they heard voices near them. He helped her up and then escorted her back to his cousin.

"I will speak to your uncle in the morning."

She smiled at him one last time.

Nathaniel escorted Lydia and his cousin Sarah to the carriage. Sarah had not wanted to leave so early, but he insisted she escort Lydia home.

"I will tell Grandmother. You will send the carriage back for her," Nathaniel said before he shut the door.

He was furious with himself for losing control with her. He wasn't ready to be married yet! He would have to speak to her uncle in the morning for certain now. If she missed her courses, he would do the honourable thing. If she wasn't with child, he would force himself to control his urges around her and wait a while longer. Who was he fooling? He would have to stay away until he knew their fate.

He went back inside Eversham's house. He needed his idiocy to be forgotten. The study was surprisingly vacant, so he took occupancy. After downing two drinks in rapid succession, he found an opium pipe on the desk, lit it and inhaled deeply.

"There you are. I wondered if you had taken your lovely goddess to the garden." Nathaniel attempted a glare at Vernon but he was so blurry it was not very effective.

"Let us not speak about her now."

"Trouble in paradise?" Vernon taunted.

"Stubble it. Hand me another pouch, would you?"

"You know, Fairmont, this is becoming a nasty habit," Vernon said as he picked up a pouch instead and reloaded Nathaniel's pipe. Nathaniel took a long, deep draw on it.

"It's shnot a habit. It's shan indulgence." His words were beginning to slur.

"Is there a difference?" Vernon replied rhetorically and went to pour himself a drink.

"Pour me another pleashe?" Nathaniel called out.

"I think you have…"

Nathaniel interrupted. "You shound like an old lady! I will get it myshelf. If I wanted a lecture, I would go home." He rose from the chair and stumbled across the room. Instead of refilling his glass, he grabbed the remainder of the bottle and helped himself.

Andrew came in to the study looking forlorn. "Have you seen Sarah?"

"Shent her home wish Ly-dya. Shouldn't have brought her dreshed like that."

Andrew looked worriedly at his cousin. "Is he foxed already?"

"Completely aped. What has happened, Abbott?" Vernon asked.

"I have just received word that my mother has passed away. I will be leaving immediately for Sussex."

"I besht come with you." He was sober enough to realize his aunt had died.

"You best leave either way," Vernon quipped. "My condolences, Abbott."

They both had to assist Nathaniel. He was too far gone to walk.

"Wait." He stopped and turned. "Fetch me that pouch." Nathaniel blinked several times, attempting to orient himself. "That was the besht shmoke I've ever had."

Vernon shook his head but reached over to retrieve the pouch for Nathaniel.

～

Nathaniel could scarcely recall what had occurred during the past week, except for what had happened in the garden with Lydia. He had found himself in Sussex at his aunt's funeral with a wretched headache, exceedingly nauseated and anxious to have another drink. When the family finally returned to London, he knew he had to speak to her uncle.

He spied the pouch from Eversham's party. He had felt different, more euphoric, yet numb that night. Andrew and Vernon had told him he was erratic and irrational, and had given him another lecture about his dissipation. He thought again of Lydia and how his lack of control had now forced his hand. He would speak to her uncle on the morrow. He could put it off no longer. But for tonight, he would open the pouch. He was going to stay at home and enjoy his last dissolute night in private.

CHAPTER 3

*N*athaniel woke, disorientated, to a dark room. His head was spinning, his mouth was dry, and he felt like the contents of his stomach would be expelled at any moment. He tried to lift his head to see where he was, but his eyes could not focus. This had been happening too often lately, waking up with a horrid headache in an unknown location. He squinted in the dim room, the only hint of light coming from the dying embers in the hearth. The room looked familiar, as if it were his father's house, not the rooms he kept.

Nathaniel rolled over and felt a leg. A lady's leg, by the feel of it, or more likely, a courtesan's. He looked down and noticed his clothing around his ankles. It was too bad he could not remember, he thought. That, too, had been happening often lately. He glanced at the lady's face to see if he recognized her. It was embarrassing not to remember these things when they met in the *ton's* drawing rooms. Ladies did not care for that.

He stumbled off the bed as he pulled his breeches up and tried to get a closer look. His head pounded and ached like never before. Perhaps he should take it easier on the opium pipe, or the whisky, he thought. He noticed the torn dress and golden curls. Strange, he did not remember having a propensity toward roughness before. He scrunched up his face. There was an odd familiarity about this female.

As he pushed back the hair from her face, he noticed the scratches all over his arms. Then he saw her face.

Nathaniel broke out in a cold sweat all over as the reality of what he had done sobered him. He immediately started retching and shaking, emptying his stomach contents until he could only heave. He sat on to the floor next to the chamber pot. How could he have done such a thing? He concentrated but could not remember any of it. Maybe there had been something else in the pipe. He shook his head. *Oh God, oh God, oh God. What do I do now?*

He rose and made his way back over to the bed. He looked at her small, frail body, disgusted with himself. Sweet little Elly. What the hell was wrong with him? Could he have been so foxed he had not noticed it was her? Had he been so foxed he had hurt a woman?

He scanned her body and did not see any serious physical injuries, thank God. Only a bad bruise to her face and bruises on her arm. *I did that to her.* How could he have hurt someone he loved? What should he do? What if she was with child? What would his father or his uncle say?

Still shaking and trying to fight back tears, he straightened Elly up as best he could, taking care to wipe the blood away. He stoked the fire, and then threw her torn gown into the flames. He put another nightgown over her head and pulled the covers over her. She did not flinch when he touched her. He hoped she would not be able to remember what happened either—for her sake.

He made his way back to his room to wash, trying to fight the panic rising inside. He would have to tell his father. It might be better to just leave—or die. It might be better just to do everyone a favour and dispose of himself before his cousin did it for him. It was impossible to keep a duel a secret, no matter what. He did not want to be a coward, but he did not want to shame Elinor further. He knew Society did not give a jot for what a Duke's heir did. Frankly, that was probably why he had wrought the path of destruction he had. But this had crossed the line, even for him. He had not been this sober in years, and he deserved whatever punishment was given to him.

Nathaniel bathed himself quickly, even more disgusted after seeing the evidence of Elly's struggle against him. He was fairly well scratched and bruised all over, and his head was splitting with the worst pain he had ever felt. He was on the verge of loading the gun and taking it to Elinor. Would she feel better then? He packed a bag of his belongings and went to face his father.

The Duke of Loring was imposing, even in his shirt sleeves and without boots. He was still in his dressing room and gave Nathaniel a surprised look at seeing his son so early in the morning.

"Just coming in for the night?" his father asked with a disapproving eyebrow. The Duke was well aware of his son's activities and reputation in Town.

"No. I did not stay out last night," Nathaniel replied sombrely.

The Duke looked at his son and, noting his unusually bleak demeanour, dismissed his valet so they could speak alone.

"What is it you have to say? Have you finally been called out by an irate father or husband?"

"Not yet." Nathaniel could not look his father in the eye.

"I see. Pack your bags. We will leave after we break our fast," the Duke said angrily.

Nathaniel looked up in surprise. His father had never suggested running away from a problem.

"I have been considering this for some time as your behaviour has declined. I had already arranged to purchase your commission, should it become necessary. I believe that time has come. We will depart soon."

"There are some that I need to make amends with first," Nathaniel said, not expecting to leave quite so suddenly.

"Then write letters. I will see them delivered. See Hastings in on your way out." He was dismissed with the wave of his father's hand.

Nathaniel nodded. Arguing would do no good, and he had not the energy. He walked by Elly's room, but she was still asleep. He went to the library and tried to write out an apology, but no words made it to the paper. How did you write, *Forgive me for violating you?*

Perhaps it was better this way. He would force his way to the front lines in battle and let Fate take its course.

∼

A few hours later, Nathaniel found himself on a packet to Portugal, bound for the Peninsular Campaign. He wondered, in a rare moment of rational thought, if he would live that long. His head was splitting; his body was shaking and sweating all over. He was immediately quarantined away from the rest of the soldiers.

"Lord Fairmont! Lord Fairmont! Can you hear me?" Someone shook Nathaniel's arm. He tried to force his eyes open, but when he did, the light seemed to cause horrible pains in his head, followed by uncontrollable bouts of retching.

"I am Dr. Craig. I am trying to help you," the doctor explained calmly.

Nathaniel managed a small nod between the violent tremors that wracked his body. He definitely needed a doctor.

"Have you been around anyone who was ill?"

He shook his head slightly.

"Do you have any idea what is wrong? Have you ever been like this before?"

"Too much." He paused for breath. "Whisky. Bad opium," he rasped.

Dr. Craig blew a frustrated breath through his lips. "How much whisky?"

"Bottles." His whole body was beginning to shake violently again. The doctor held him down until the seizing passed.

"This is not good. We are going to have to wean you off slowly. Otherwise, you will most surely die."

Nathaniel shook his head in vehement protest. "No more. Never again."

"You could die. It will get worse than this," the doctor said, adamant.

"Then let me die. It was my fault."

"What was your fault?" Dr. Craig tried to understand.

"I hurt her. I did that to her. I deserve this!" Lord Fairmont began jabbering deliriously. He continued talking nonsense and lost consciousness. Dr. Craig gave him some small amounts of laudanum and alcohol to help with the tremors and wean him off his dependence. Lord Fairmont was in bad condition and would likely die if he stopped taking those substances suddenly. When he was through the worst, they could discuss stopping for good.

This was Dr. Craig's first patient as an army physician, and how fortunate to get a spoiled, drunken lord, his first case on a long journey by sea. He had never treated anyone for acute withdrawal before, but he had studied this in school in Edinburgh. Studying and doing were two completely different animals. Watching this man suffer was akin to watching a mad dog.

Hallucinations, drenching sweats, veins pounding in his neck and shaking were just the beginning of what this young lord had to look forward to in order to conquer his demons—and more, from the sound of it.

Lydia had waited and waited that next morning for Nathaniel to arrive to speak with her uncle. But he never came. She wanted to be sick. She wanted to believe he was different, that his love had been real. She would be shunned if anyone found out. She had been warned, hadn't she? If only she had understood what a rake truly was.

She had learned that Nathaniel's aunt had passed away. He had left immediately for the country to attend the funeral. But then he still did not come. Weeks later a letter arrived, after she heard he had purchased a commission and left for the Peninsula.

Lydia lurched for the basin. Sick again. How long would this stomach ailment last?

Her maid handed her a wet cloth and took the basin away. She curled up on the bed. Maybe she would waste away and die. She could not see what there was left to live for.

Meggie came back into the room to replace the basin.

"Forgive me for speakin' so, my lady, but is there a chance you might be....increasing?"

"I do not know how I could be gaining weight when I have not held anything down for weeks."

"No, I don't mean it like that." She wrinkled her face and looked down. "I mean a baby, my lady."

Lydia froze. Oh, dear God. She subconsciously touched her abdomen. Why had she not considered? She had read of such things in books. She had been so distraught, she had not realized.

"Meggie? How...how would I know?"

"Well, if you were with a man..." The maid glanced at Lydia's pale face and likely knew the answer.

"Then you miss your courses..." She had.

"Then you get the morning sickness." The final nail in the coffin.

And Nathaniel was nowhere to be found. Lydia threw her face in her hands. Would he come back if he knew? Did it matter? His letter had said *not to wait for him. He did not know when he would return. She would be better off without him.*

She had to be sick again.

"What am I going to do?"

"Shall I fetch your aunt, my lady? She might know of a doctor who can give you a cordial. I know mistresses..."

"No!" Lydia said vehemently. "I need time to think. You may go now." She didn't have time. She knew it only took a few months for a woman's belly to grow round with child. But the thought of destroying the life inside her... No. She held on to the place where her child grew. She only had one option if Nathaniel did not want her: to marry someone else.

❧

Lydia set out on her mission when she realized Nathaniel was not coming back. She had learned much from her brief foray into courtship, mainly what made a man want a woman. She'd honed the skills of flirting, teasing and acting the coquette. Plenty of men took notice... including her uncle.

"Lydia, dear," he said as he knocked quietly and entered. Why was he in her room? He had never entered her room before. She pulled her coverlet tighter.

"Yes, Uncle Dannon?"

"I think we need to have a little discussion about your change in behaviour." He sat on the edge of her bed.

Drat.

"You are beginning to attract the wrong type of attention. You will not be able to contract an eligible match if you act in such a fashion. I know you are bruised from your *affaire* with Fairmont, but you still have much to recommend you." He looked her over in a way that gave her the chills.

"I do not care whom I marry," she said blandly.

"Pardon?"

"Do you know of anyone seeking a match which you could arrange?" she said as unemotionally as she could.

He narrowed his eyes at her. "Why the sudden indifference?"

She shrugged. "I find I no longer care for the idea of love."

He looked at her long and hard. She could see him thinking. And then he came to the correct conclusion.

"I thought I had heard you retching in the morning. Is it Fairmont's?"

She felt as if she'd been slapped. He had to ask? She couldn't bear to look up.

"And he is long gone." He sighed. "You should have been clever enough to get the ring on your finger first. If you want to act like Haymarket ware, you might as well pay your shot here."

Did he mean? She looked up with wide eyes. She looked at him with revulsion.

"You will see Dr. Tinsley in the morning. I am not raising your bastard child, too."

"No! I will not let you hurt this baby," she said with fierce determination.

"Why do you care? He won't want you when he comes back, and no one else will have you when they know. A fine marriage you will have when your husband discovers you have thrust someone else's bastard on to him!" he said angrily.

"Send me away then! Just do not hurt the baby. I will give it up. Please, just do not hurt the baby." She was down on her knees, grovelling and crying.

He looked down on her in disgust.

"One condition."

"Anything. I will do anything," she pleaded.

"I will send you to the country to rusticate. But you will do as I ask, and it will stay between you and me."

She nodded. She was desperate, but she never could have imagined what was coming. As he helped her up, he let his hands roam.

"What are you doing?"

"I'm receiving payment for my troubles. You made a deal," he said through gritted teeth.

"No!" she screamed defiantly.

She felt a hard slap across her face that sent her backwards onto the bed. She was afraid to look up, afraid of what she would see.

"Have you changed your mind? Because your only other option is to leave my house for good."

She would not let him take her baby. She began to shake with fear, knowing that she had no choice. One mistake, and her life as she knew it was over.

CHAPTER 4

SIX YEARS LATER, FEBRUARY 1814

The Roman Camp, Orthez, France

*L*ieutenant Colonel Fairmont, Major Adam Trowbridge and Major Andrew Abbott sat around their shared quarters in south-west France, mindlessly playing cards in the post-victory haze, and awaiting marching orders from their commander. General Lord Wellington, or Hookey, as he was affectionately known to them, was nicknamed for his prominent proboscis.

Their childhood friend, Rhys, along with Adam and Andrew, were all members of the General's staff and spent most of their time running dispatches from place to place. Nathaniel, Lord Fairmont, had refused the safer position, placing himself on the front lines and fighting like his nickname—Achilles—himself. He had advanced quickly through the ranks, despite his protests, and now found himself a Lieutenant Colonel of the 7th Hussars Regiment. He was recovering from a sabre wound to his leg, received during the day's battle at Orthez, and had been ordered to convalesce, or he would not be with them now.

"That was a famous advance by the 7th, Nate," Adam reflected.

"Aye. It was tough terrain for most of the mounts. I even wondered a time or two if your men would make it," Andrew quipped.

"I did not doubt for a moment," Nathaniel said without arrogance.

"The other Hussars cried off, yet you rode neck or nothing up the ridge." Andrew shook his head in bewilderment.

"It was not neck or nothing. Salty knew exactly what to do." Nathaniel threw out a random card onto the table. *Salty* was his trusted charger, named for the white spots scattered on his grey coat.

"You let your horse determine your advances?" Adam questioned Nathaniel's madness.

"Animals know. He has not led me wrong thus far." Nathaniel shrugged off his reasoning. "My men were even able to round up over two hundred French *diables bleus* while Soult was making his escape."

"Well, something you did frightened them. They blew up the bridge behind them to keep Achilles away," Andrew said, as he watched Adam play the card he seemed to hope his partner was holding.

"I miss Rhys. You make a horrid card partner, Nate," Andrew said, as he threw the cards down on the makeshift table. Rhys, now Lord Vernon, had recently left the campaign to take over the Earldom upon his father's death. Nathaniel's trusted batman, Ajax, so-called to parry Nathaniel's Achilles, made up their fourth player in Rhys's absence. He was a man of few words but had been a fierce warrior before his injuries.

Nathaniel shrugged and lit a cheroot. "We cannot all be good at everything. I will stick to fighting, and you stick to being a delivery boy—and card games," Nathaniel said dryly.

Andrew threw the nearest available object—an empty pannikin—at Nathaniel's head, which he ducked smoothly. The movement caused Nathaniel to wince as a pain shot through his wounded leg.

"You are making my point for me in a most excellent fashion," he retorted.

"Have some cognac? This is a mighty fine vintage the Foot has managed to barter for. The Frogs at least know how to do drink properly." Andrew held a pannikin out to his cousin.

Nathaniel shook his head in refusal.

"Even for pain? It is admirable you have stopped drinking and such like, but I would think a sword to the leg a valid reason." Andrew waved his hand. "Medicinal use and all that."

"It is too slippery a slope."

"Suit yourself. You seem to have the luck of the devil, anyway. I took you for a dead man when I saw the *Cuirassier* charge directly toward you. He should have had the advantage of you from his position."

"Hookey has the devil's own luck, too. Never seen him unseated before," Adam added.

"Is he injured?" Nathaniel asked, this the first he had heard of Wellington's being hit.

"Only bruised. Canister shot hit his sword hilt. And here you are with little more than a scratch," Adam remarked.

"The fool could not handle his mount," Nathaniel said calmly, "or he would have easily hit the mark."

"No one handles their horseflesh like you, Nate. I will give you that. But do you have to risk yourself like a deuced wild animal in every battle?" Andrew chided again.

Nathaniel was saved from answering when a young lance-corporal knocked and entered the room with the post. Mail was sporadic at best, if it ever even made it to them, but was the highlight of their month when received. "Sir, for you." He handed a packet of letters to Andrew, whose father and sisters wrote to him tirelessly.

"And for you, sir." He handed a dispatch to Adam.

"And for you, sir." He handed a letter to Nathaniel. He looked at the letter with surprise. He only received dispatches, never letters.

The young corporal saluted and left, and Nathaniel gingerly fingered the paper before sliding his finger under the familiar wax seal to open it. It had to be bad news.

The friends sat quietly reading their letters. Andrew, probably reading the tales of his sister's adventures in America, and his father's diplomatic efforts to end the war between England and America.

Adam silently read of his brother, Max, and his continued depravity, and his father's despair of him ever settling down and producing an heir. He moved on to the dispatch from Wellington; he was needed in the effort against the Americans. He would sail on the next ship, leaving in one week's time, he looked up to mention.

Nathaniel read the missive from his father, then read it again. His father wanted him to return. *"...Your return is long overdue... you have proven yourself reformed...a hero...a son I am proud of... time to take up your duties as heir in England."* The same phrases kept repeating themselves over and over. A sickening feeling overcame him. If his father only knew.

Nathaniel stepped outside the tent. He needed some fresh air to quell the panic. He lit another cheroot and took a deep draw to calm himself. Just the thought of returning to England sent his anxiety level soaring. He had learned to master his excesses of drink and opium, but never a day passed that he did not feel their effects and cravings for them, especially when facing this. He would rather face Napoleon's fiercest than return to England. At least he knew Elinor lived in America now. She and his uncle Charles had left the same day he had, according to his cousin, Andrew. To Nathaniel's knowledge, no one else knew of his disgrace, save himself and possibly Elinor. If she remembered, she had not told anyone.

Even if no one else ever knew, it was enough that he did. And now, he was a hardened soldier through and through. He had fought with nothing to lose, yet God would not show him mercy. He had seen and done things on the battlefield that no one this side of hell should have to experience. He could only welcome it as his penance. He sighed.

Perhaps he could visit when the campaign was over, but until then his father would have to wait. The Duke would never understand what being a soldier truly meant. None of Society would. But Nathaniel knew he would not fit into that life any longer. He was not capable of forgiving or forgetting the monster he was.

Months later, Boney had been captured, and Nathaniel could no longer delay the inevitable. He stepped out of a coach in London. He stood on the pavement and looked around. It was a rush of the past slapping him in the face. He inhaled deeply…and was immediately overcome with sorrow. England was home. However, it reminded him of everything he despised about himself, everything he had single-handedly destroyed.

Six years. He shook the regret away momentarily and paid off the driver, taking his small valise. He had parted with his batman in Dover, wanting to face London alone and allow Ajax to visit his family.

Ajax came from excellent stock, but as a younger son of a squire, he had enlisted to lessen the burden on his family. When he had been injured, heroically saving other members of their regiment, Nathaniel had kept him on to prevent his being sent home. His face was badly burned, as were his hands, and one of his legs had been so severely injured that it often dragged behind him when he became tired. He had not been home since being injured and was nervous about his reception. Nathaniel knew Ajax did not like to be away from him, but he wanted no one near to witness this.

Nathaniel walked along Pall Mall toward The Guards' Club, taking rooms where he would not have to maintain a Society façade. Anonymity and blowing clouds were Nathaniel's planned coping mechanism for a time. He would sneak out for walks or stare out of the window toward the square. Long hair, several days' beard and plain clothing allowed him a chance to re-acclimatize to the city without being recognized. He was more comfortable in that role, and he fought daily with himself, trying to muster up enough courage to step into Loring Place.

Ever since he had set foot onto English soil, the nightmares had once again pervaded his sleep. Every time he closed his eyes he saw the vision of golden curls and innocence marred, as he had left Elinor that fateful morning. He still could not remember doing those horrible acts to her, and his imagination feared the worst. He would drift off into fitful slumber, only to awaken terrorized and drenched in sweat. His night terrors were combinations of fierce battles to the death, where Elinor's face would take the place of the soldier he was fighting. Or he would come upon a soldier violating a woman and pull the man furiously away, only to find it was himself.

He stood in front of the glass, looking at the unfamiliar man staring back at him. It had been years since he had studied himself in such a way. Lines and scars marked his weather-tanned face. The only familiar sight was his haunted grey eyes, loathing him in reflection.

His solicitor had sent a note around from his father; he was expected home for a ball. He would do the pretty, then escape as soon as he was able. He forced himself to leave his rooms and procure the proper evening dress. He would not wear his regimentals; the uniform garnered undue attention, and his father expected him to have sold out. He was not prepared to do any such thing, but he hoped to obtain his father's blessing before sailing again. Wellington had given him leave to 'do what he must'.

He made his way toward Bond Street to procure the necessary items for a temporary re-emergence into Society. This was his first foray out amongst the polite world since his arrival. The crowds and noise unsettled him. The loud crack of a whip or slammed door and he was ducking for cover, automatically reaching for his sabre with one hand and his pistol with the other; every person was a potential threat.

He had skulked about the fringes, only stopping to converse with wounded veterans reduced to penury and help them find shelter. He was filled with disgust at the treatment the brave soldiers were receiving on their return. He vowed to lessen their plight somehow. There had to be some advantage to being heir to a dukedom. He certainly did not have need for his exorbitant allowance; he would see it put to a worthy cause.

He became distracted, considering how he would help these wounded soldiers, and did not notice the commotion up ahead. He was upon the horde before he realized what was happening. At the centre of the mêlée was a man being kicked and punched, as vulgarities were hurled from all directions. Despite his desire for anonymity,

Colonel Fairmont presented himself with a deep booming voice, leaving no doubt he expected to be obeyed.

"Cease and desist!"

The leader stopped and the crowd parted enough for Nathaniel to approach. They did not disperse, waiting to see if any further action would be taken.

"At once!"

The mob began to scatter a bit as many realized they had lost control and checked themselves. The leader of the brawl stood defiantly challenging Nathaniel to enforce justice himself. Nathaniel glanced toward the man lying face down on the ground and wondered why he did not remove himself when he had the chance. He must have been beaten badly before he had arrived. The leader balled his fists, clearly eager for more. Nathaniel would like nothing better than to exert his frustrations on this sorry excuse for humanity, but this was hardly the place he had to continuously remind himself.

"What offence has this man committed against you?"

The crowd recognized a gentleman and thus stayed nearby, eager for more fighting.

"Look at him! He is not fit to be in public view. There is a place where they send monsters such as he!" The man took the beaten man's foot and cruelly flipped him over. The crowd had grown to considerable proportions and now included ladies and children. Several gasps of indignation sounded and Nathaniel glanced at the man, only to find his loyal batman at his feet.

Anyone who had spent any time on the battlefield with Colonel Fairmont knew that flash of his grey eyes and would have run halfway to Scotland before looking back.

"You are not worthy to walk upon the ground he spits on," Nathaniel said in his deadly voice. Before the instigator had the chance for reply, Nathaniel had levelled the scum out with one hit. He called for the constable and began to scoop up the injured Ajax. The crowd parted in awe.

"Make sure he does not leave without the constable's escort," Nathaniel directed some nearby men.

"No chance of that, Fairmont. The rogue will be lucky to see daylight again after that hit," a familiar voice said.

He was joined by Lord Vernon, who had recognized Nathaniel, despite his long hair and beard. The old friends carried Ajax to the nearest hackney.

Vernon climbed in after directing the driver to his town-house.

"Much obliged, Vernon."

Vernon acknowledged with a nod. Nathaniel quickly scanned his retainer for injuries and ascertained his wounds were likely no more than bruises, as surmised by his groans when prodded.

"Rather dramatic way to announce your homecoming, Fairmont. I will see to Ajax. You had best present yourself in Audley Street before word reaches Loring, though you are fortunate the distinguished gathering did not take you for a wild beast yourself," Vernon said sardonically, casting a glance at his old friend.

"In my defence, I was on my way to procure clothing," Nathaniel retorted.

"And a razor, one would hope."

Nathaniel ignored this barb. "Would you be so kind as to have a doctor look him over?"

"Naturally."

"He must have been on his way to find me. I wish he had sent word ahead." He sighed. "Quite the civil stock we hail from."

This was met with a rude snort.

Four-and-twenty. Lady Lydia was becoming desperate. She had resigned herself long ago to the idea that Nathaniel was never coming back to her. He had sent a letter stating as much six years ago, but she could no longer take performing the unspeakable acts her uncle and guardian demanded as payment for silence. She was only tolerated amongst the *ton* because of him, he reminded her daily. A few more months.

Nathaniel had filled Lydia's ears with promises, and she'd had no experience or warning of the power of handsome rakes, having lost her mother young. Raised by her aunt, who had paid little heed to Lydia, her only efforts were exerted on her own person. Lydia had loved Nathaniel in earnest, hopeful to find the affection she craved in such a desirable form.

When Nathaniel had left for the army, and Lydia had found herself increasing, she had thrown herself at nearly every eligible bachelor in hopes of finding a father for her unborn child. Her reputation was ruined anyway if discovered; it was her only hope. She had managed to be compromised by not a soul. No one dared dangle after Lord Fairmont's marked territory.

Her reputation became known as fast; she was no good to eligible bachelors, save for flirtations. Even the rakes would do no more than flirt, afraid her uncle would make them pay. Lydia had foreseen his wish to dispose of the babe, and had arranged for her old nurse to take the child, and the money Uncle had intended to 'donate' to the foundling home, to care for it. Most of her pin money was also sent to care for the infant. She had become skilled at making over old gowns, and managed on letters of her daughter's well-being and once or twice-yearly visits.

She would be five-and-twenty soon, with no prospects. She would be free from her uncle's guardianship and would have a small competence to survive on. However, she would not come into her full inheritance until she either married or she reached thirty years of age. She longed to be with her daughter. She had grown up motherless, and wanted nothing more than the relationship she had been denied. Not a day went by that she did not think of her little Amelia, with her father's grey eyes and blonde locks. She had often dreamt of Nathaniel returning from war and the three of them living happily as a family. Lydia knew these to be air dreams; six years ago she had mourned the loss of her love, her daughter, and endured the sadistic punishment of her guardian. She had nowhere else to go, and only a thin barrier lay between desperation and knowing how she might be together with her daughter again.

She made her way to Bond Street. She would have to scrape and order a new ball gown, for the Duke of Loring was presenting his niece to Society. Rumour held she was a diamond of the first water. Lydia fumed. She needed no more competition for the bachelors! She would have to take desperate measures, she decided, for time was running out. She would look over the new débutantes at the Queen's tea that afternoon. She felt sure Lady Beatrice would be a fount of information. It was ironic, she had been so long a part of the *ton*, she and Nathaniel's sister had become friends. Beatrice at least remembered when Nathaniel had courted her and still held out hope that he would return for her.

Lydia exited the *modiste's* shop after ordering the most daring gown she could. She stopped dead in her tracks and did not notice the rude comments and stares she received from passers-by. She had seen a ghost—one that looked like *him*. She shook her head and blinked away tears. She must stop imagining Nathaniel around every corner. He was never coming back for her and the child he knew nothing about.

She stood there dazed until her carriage pulled in front of the shop to take her home. She continued to be disturbed by the vision of Nathaniel she had seen. Once home, she pulled out their old letters, and his lock of hair that she'd held onto, almost identical in colour to their daughter's. She looked at the sketch of Amelia she had made the last time she had seen her. It was like Nathaniel looking directly at her through his daughter's eyes. Why had she not appealed to the Duke when she found herself increasing? For her daughter's sake, that's why. Amelia would have been termed a bastard and taken away to the foundling home.

A knock sounded on her door. She hurriedly stashed her mementos before the door opened. Her uncle stood before her with that look on his face.

"Lydia, I see you have been naughty again," he said in his patronizing manner.

Oh, dear Lord, what could it be this time? She looked at him enquiringly, trying to brace herself for what she knew was coming. He was normally sitting in the Lords at this time of day, so she had not been careful to lock her door.

"Madame Bissette sent a bill for a new ball gown." He held up the damning evidence.

"That should not have been sent to you, Uncle. I was intending to pay for it."

"Now Lydia, you know I am not such a nip-cheese as to begrudge you a new gown," he said as he walked closer, loosening his cravat.

"No, sir. I did not mean to imply—" She dared not argue. She was still smarting from the first time she had refused him.

"Shh," he interrupted her with a finger to her lips. "All I require is a few moments of your time. Nothing more than you did for your lover. At least I give you clothing and shelter. I will not abandon you as he did. Now there's a good girl."

CHAPTER 5

$\mathcal{N}$athaniel had received any number of honours for his bravery in the field, but he was trying to find enough courage to enter his childhood home. He had not mustered the nerve before today, but he could delay no longer since the ball was tonight. He forced his feet up the stairs to the door of Loring Place.

Now or never. He lifted the knocker and let it drop. The door was opened quickly. Barnes, the long-time butler, showed nary a flicker of emotion as he held it wide for Master Nathaniel. The prodigal son had returned at last.

"Hallo, Barnes. I trust you are well?"

"Yes, my lord. Welcome home, my lord. We have been anticipating your arrival for some time. His Grace will be most pleased."

"Where might I find my father at this hour?"

"I believe he is still in the library, my lord."

"Thank you, Barnes. It is nice to see you looking well."

"And yourself, my lord."

Nathaniel made his way to the library and knocked softly on the door, inhaling the familiar scents of his childhood home. Little had changed.

"Enter," the Duke boomed in his business-like voice.

Nathaniel could not help but smile. He had missed his family and all of their quirks, despite everything. He stood quietly inside the door as he had as a child. He acknowledged he was far from that fresh-faced young lad, but he was not sure how his father would view his presence—despite the invitation. He remained where he was and stood silently until the Duke looked up from his task.

When the Duke registered who stood before him, he barely forced out, in a whisper, "Nathaniel?"

"'Tis I, Father," Nathaniel said quietly.

The two men met in the middle of the room in a warm embrace, both too overcome for words. The Duke continued to hold his son long past the point of comfort.

"I am sorry, my son. I cannot seem to believe you are here in the flesh," he said, releasing his grip when he seemed to realize he had been holding Nathaniel too tight. He stepped away and took a long look at his heir.

"Was your trip comfortable?" He gestured for Nathaniel to take a seat.

"More comfortable than being shot at and bivouacking in a cold rain," Nathaniel said good-humouredly.

The Duke appeared shocked by his words. Did he really not know what army life was like?

"I am happy you made it in time for Elinor's presentation ball tonight."

Nathaniel's chest tightened. No. Perhaps his father had misspoken. Let it be another Elinor.

"Elinor?" He barely managed to speak the name out loud.

"Your cousin?" his father prompted.

"Andrew said they lived in America now."

"Aye, and they were forced to leave when the fighting reached the shores of their home."

Of course. Why did he not consider such an eventuality? He should never have left the Continent.

"May I get you a drink? I am sure the journey has been tiring," the Duke asked as he rose to pour drinks.

"No. Thank you, Father." He would not mention he had been in Town for weeks.

The Duke raised an inquisitive eyebrow but said nothing. He turned and helped himself.

"I expected you sooner. It has been months since Napoleon was sent to Elba."

"There is always business to be tidied up."

"You must be invaluable to Wellesley," the Duke said somewhat sarcastically as he reverted to Wellington's surname. "The rest of your regiment returned some time ago."

Nathaniel had only been listening with half an ear. He had been staring into the fire, pondering his dilemma. "Oh, yes. I volunteered to stay behind and help."

The Duke stared at his son.

"I was not ready to return yet," Nathaniel answered honestly.

The Duke chose not to be offended, and acted as if he was grateful that he was here.

The two remained closeted thus for several hours, the Duke continuing to ask questions, Nathaniel trying to concentrate on his answers. The entire time, Nathaniel felt trepidation building inside him. He had imagined facing Elinor over and over in his nightmares, but he still had not found a way to beg forgiveness satisfactorily. He was still unsure if she had any recollection of that horrid night, but he feared the worst.

The clock struck seven and the Duke realized the time.

"I must make haste. Our dinner guests are due to arrive. I will make excuses for you, but do be down in time for the receiving line." The Duke gave Nathaniel another crushing hug before he departed.

Nathaniel nodded, still too shocked to think clearly. He wanted to escape out of the front door and as far away from England as he could go. But he knew the time had come when he could run no more.

He walked the familiar path to his old rooms. In some ways he felt like he had never been away. But in other ways he felt like he had been absent for an eternity. His room was just as he remembered: his old things were on his dresser just as he'd left them, the counterpane unchanged, the familiar scent of sandalwood. He spied a full decanter and froze. He had not been so tempted to have a drink since the first week of his abstinence.

He stood there for several minutes before walking over to the bottle. His hand came up within reach and shook as he fought the inner battle to have a drink. Only one, his conscience told him. He did not know if he could face Elinor in his right mind. He poured the amber liquid into the glass. He swirled it around and inhaled the familiar peaty smell.

Oh, how he longed to pour the liquid fire down his throat and soothe his anxieties away. He threw the glass into the fire and reached over and pulled the bell. A servant appeared quickly.

"Please remove this and see that no more enters this room," he said rather curtly.

"Yes, my lord." The boy bowed nervously and rushed out the room with the offending decanter.

Nathaniel slumped into the nearby chair and buried his face in his hands. His shoulders began to shake, and he wept until a servant knocked and entered with a fresh bath and another with a tray.

He looked up to find Ajax limping toward him to ready him for the ball.

"What is the meaning of this? You should be in bed," Nathaniel asked, concerned.

"I'm much obliged to you and the Major for coming to my assistance, but I will not lie in bed any longer. My services are needed." He readied the bath and stared at Nathaniel until he complied.

"You were ordered to take a holiday," Nathaniel said sternly.

"I could not stand to hear my mama cry. She could not bear the sight of me," he replied without showing emotion.

"I am sorry, Ajax. I, for one, am deuced happy to see your face."

The loyal batman simply nodded and pulled out the razor.

He was shaved and clothed in the latest mode. The famous Weston had been all too pleased to oblige the heir to the Duke of Loring for the right price. He pulled his long blonde hair back into a queue, instead of the more fashionable crops favoured by most military men. He was physically presentable at least.

Time for battle.

～

One look. The instant his eyes locked with Elinor's, he knew. The feeling was indescribable—worse than waking up and realizing what he had done to her. More than anything, he wanted to speak to her and beg forgiveness. The timing could not be worse. Would he have made the effort to speak to her before had he known she was in London? The question was better left unanswered. But seeing her face and the pain in her eyes made him vow to do anything possible to right his atrocities against her.

"Cousin."

"Nathaniel."

He was stopped short by a cold glare and curt reply from his grandmother. Evidently she was also aware of his transgressions.

He stood in the receiving line and made polite greetings. He scarcely remembered most of these people after six years, and the last place on earth he wished to be was a Society ballroom. His mind was occupied with what to do and say to Elinor. Perhaps leaving her alone was for the best. He would try to speak to his grandmother before approaching Elinor again.

He longed to slip away and formulate a plan, for he doubted not that this would be his fiercest crusade yet. However, returning home after six years, a decorated war hero and titled bachelor, made his wishes moot. Fortunately, his father swept Elinor away for the opening dance, and he was surrounded by familiar faces before the mamas got their claws into him.

Nathaniel spent the dance becoming reacquainted with his oldest friends. He had not been asked to stand up with his mother or sister as yet, and was relieved by the short reprieve. His cousin, Andrew

Abbott; Rhys, now Lord Vernon, and Adam, now Lord Easton, apprised him of the happenings in the American War, and he told of how he left Lord Wellington. He was taken completely by surprise when his father led Elinor straight to him and gave him her hand. He saw her hesitation. For a moment he thought all would be exposed right there in the middle of the ballroom. Andrew became instantly hostile, reaching for Elinor and telling her she did not have to dance with him. Vernon and Easton cast him looks of enquiry but remained quiet. How many others knew?

He took Elinor's trembling hand and led her out to the dance floor. Thankfully, it was not a waltz, so their interaction was minimal. She instantly requested that he not ask her to speak right now.

"Very well. I cannot blame you for feeling that way," he responded quietly.

Every step, every breath was agony. He spent the entire dance debating ending it all, but that would have been too easy, undeserved. For six years he had risked everything, hoping he could at least do some good for his country, and that God would choose to take his damned soul over the innocent ones. Instead, here he was inflicting more pain on someone he loved. Could he ever make things right for her?

"I know my presence here is distressing to you. Only say the word and I will leave again."

Elinor remained silent and avoided looking at him. The dance ended, but before he could let her go he had to speak the words. He could not know if he would have another chance. As he led Elinor back to her brother, he whispered, "I am sorry."

"This is not over, Nate." Andrew was fuming. Nathaniel nodded and kept walking toward the terrace for some fresh air.

Lady Lydia arrived late to the ball. Her uncle was still demanding special favours for having bought her a new gown while her aunt waited patiently downstairs for them to finish. She swallowed the bile that rose in her throat as she watched him and her aunt present themselves as Society's finest. She longed to end this charade, to stop pretending and be with her Amelia. She had almost lost hope of finding love again, but she must find a way to support herself and her daughter before it was too late.

The receiving line was closed and the dancing had already commenced. Lady Beatrice had informed her Nathaniel was to be here when she'd seen her at the débutante tea. She had not seen a ghost, but the real Nathaniel that day. Two weeks of fretting over her appearance and what she would say to him, looking for him around every corner. She was nervous and giddy simultaneously. Her future and their daughter's rested on his reception—and his belief—of her.

Lydia glanced around the ballroom and finally spotted his imposing form a head above the rest—dancing with his beautiful cousin, Elinor. She wanted to be sick. She had tried to rid herself of her obsession with him for six years. She had looked in the daily papers for news of his heroics and rise through the ranks without fail. She knew every battle almost by heart. Seeing him again tonight undid her resolve to be unaffected. He was stunning. Her heart raced and her hands trembled with anticipation. This man was no longer the tall, slim buck she had fallen in love with. He had filled out his clothing to perfection, as only a man who spent hours in the saddle could. His golden hair was long and his face was harsh, but his eyes were the same piercing, stormy grey.

How would he receive her? She had also changed much. Having a child had changed her figure in such ways that men thought her only fit for one thing, and her uncle would not allow her to forget it. She was past the first blush of youth, though still handsome, she supposed. She knew she had garnered a loose reputation, as her hypocritical aunt loved to remind her. "Pretty is as pretty does, Lydia." She had learned from the master.

Her resolve faltered upon seeing Nathaniel; she began to question her plan. Had he found someone else? Would he hear of her reputation and want nothing to do with her? That would be the ultimate indignity if he were to shun her after she'd given her innocence to him. He had made her promises and she had trusted him. How was she to know he would be sent away to the army? She was no longer a gullible innocent, but she had to survive.

Lady Beatrice approached her and she put her mask in place.

"Are you going to stand here and gape all night? I collect you are also in raptures over Nathaniel's return. The ballroom is positively buzzing with the return of the country's biggest hero next to Wellington."

Lydia began to deny that she had been staring at Nathaniel, but knew Beatrice would see right through her. "At least it takes the attention away from your dearest cousin," she replied in her practised society voice.

Both of them glanced maliciously at Elinor, who was surrounded by a herd of bachelors.

"I have plans to put a stop to her reign," Beatrice said confidently. "But for now we must reacquaint you and Nathaniel. Come. There will be a waltz soon."

Lydia was led abruptly toward Nathaniel and found herself momentarily at a loss for words or affectations. She stood before him and he took her breath away. Here stood the father of her child.

She prayed he recognized her, and that she had meant something to him in the past. She could not bring herself to act with him, her raw emotion no doubt writ upon her face. She forced herself to steel her nerves, despite her heart warring within her. She could not afford to give in when her daughter's—their daughter's— welfare was at stake. She stood there taking in every detail.

"You remember Lady Lydia, do you not, Nathaniel?" Beatrice asked mockingly.

"How could I forget? My lady." Nathaniel bowed and kissed her proffered hand.

"My lord." She curtsied.

The orchestra began the promised waltz.

"Do not let me keep you from dancing. I see my next partner approaching." Beatrice was unsubtly suggesting Nathaniel partner her. It would have been preferable had he suggested the dance himself, but beggars could not be choosers. She would have a moment in his arms again, however obtained. He held out his arm to her and led her to the floor.

Lady Lydia—another source of his shame, Nathaniel reflected. She looked more stunning than ever with her alabaster skin highlighted by her dark locks, and a daring burgundy silk dress that looked moulded to her now buxom figure. She was a real woman now, not his shy first love. He scoffed. His only love. And he had loved her, despite the light-skirts and path of destruction he had wrought upon himself in the name of acquiring town bronze. He'd had good intentions, but had been too wild to settle at that time. He would have done his duty should it have become necessary, but that would have been another disaster—albeit preferable to the one in which he now found himself. He'd had no doubt of receiving permission when the timing was right, but now it was never to be. He dared not let himself entertain feelings again. There was no chance of their happiness. He only hoped she had been able to continue her life.

He took her in his arms and felt a momentary softening of his cold heart. How he wished things were different! One disgusting act had forever damned his soul and any chance of future peace. He forcibly hardened his heart again, for he dared not toy with either of their affections. He found himself at a loss for the proper words. An awkward silence fell between them, neither knowing where to begin.

"How are you, Lord Fairmont?" she eventually asked, as if they had been mere social acquaintances.

"I am well, thank you," he answered too politely. "And yourself?"

"Well enough. Are you pleased to be back?" She looked up at him shyly.

He hesitated. "No."

She forced a small laugh. "Very well, I beg you do not sweeten your answer for my benefit."

He still had enough decency to try to look sheepish. He had

forgotten how to speak with anyone other than soldiers. "I beg your pardon. It was not my intention to be churlish. I am unfit for a ballroom."

"Nonsense. You look extremely fit."

A smile broke through involuntarily. There was a glimpse of his Lydia. *His Lydia*. Silence ensued for a length of the floor before Lydia spoke.

"Nathaniel, I need to speak to you."

"You can say what needs to be said now."

"I cannot. We must speak soon," she paused, "about us." Her voice betrayed a tinge of desperation which she quickly hid.

"You need to forget me. There can be no us." He saw her flinch as he led her toward the side of the ballroom.

"I am afraid that is quite impossible." She gave a small curtsy, as her lip began to tremble, and exited out of the door.

Nathaniel watched Lydia walk away and fought back every urge to run after her. He could see the hurt in her eyes. He wondered what she needed to speak to him about. What had her life been like these past years? He had promised her marriage and she was obviously still unwed. Had she waited for him? Had their indiscretion made her unmarriageable?

He needed to get out of this ballroom and soon. His anxiety was reaching its limit and he was suffocating. There were spirits every-where, and it took every ounce of restraint not to take a glass. He tugged at his cravat and fought the urge to pull it off. Seeing Lydia and Elinor again within the span of two hours, knowing how many lives he had destroyed, caused him to reflect on what value *his* life actually held. He was good at killing people on the battlefield—quite the redeeming quality. He had ruined Elinor's life, his own life, and very possibly Lydia's too.

He made his way to the nearest point of escape, but was stopped short by his father.

"Is everything all right, Nathaniel?" the Duke asked with concern.

"Beg pardon, Father. I need some fresh air. This is a bit over-whelming."

"No need to explain, my son. Please, if you need anything..."

Nathaniel nodded.

"Will you be staying with us?"

Nathaniel saw the desperation in his father's eyes. He never wanted to cross the threshold of this house again, but he could not resist the pleading eyes of the Duke. There was no guise of manipulation or threats as there had been years ago. His father genuinely wanted him there.

"I am only out for a walk, Father. I will return soon." He tried to smile and reassure his father.

Relief flooded the Duke's face, and he nodded and stepped out of the way for him to pass.

Lydia escaped from the ballroom and headed straight for the door. She had Barnes call for her uncle's carriage and asked the stoic butler to convey the message to her aunt that she was not feeling well. She managed to fight back the sobs that were crowding her chest until the footman closed the door. How could one dance undo all of her resolve? She had tried for six years to forget him. He had asked how she had been. *Never better.* How do you tell of six years of torment? How could she broach the unspeakable? For a moment she had caught a flash of the old Nathaniel, but he had quickly reverted to a distant, cold stranger. She fought to control her tears. Her uncle's home was not far enough away to gain composure. She ran into the house and up the stairs, and locked the door to her room.

She had to stay strong; it was only a few more weeks until she could escape this hell forever. She knew now that there was no hope for Nathaniel and her. The dance had told her everything she needed to know: she was unwanted. But she suddenly had no desire to marry any other. He was not even interested in the one thing she was good at, she thought ironically; the mistake that had her in dire straits. She would not give Amelia up, no matter what. Unfortunately, she still needed Nathaniel's help to support their daughter. She wished there were another way. If he would help her, then she would not have to sell her body and soul to survive. She would move with Amelia and Nurse to parts unknown and set herself up as a widow and forget him. It was almost her birthday; the end was in sight. She only had to find a way to speak to him and plead her case.

CHAPTER 6

*T*he only times Nathaniel had had an entire night of sleep in the past six years were after a battle, when his body had succumbed due to pure exhaustion. Scarcely a night would pass otherwise that he did not awake haunted by the eyes of those he had harmed in battle—or Elinor's.

He had become a prisoner to his sins. There was no escape, even in sleep; he was afraid to close his eyes. Never a day or night would pass when he would stop trying to change the outcome. And while he longed to lose consciousness and escape from himself for good, he knew that there was one who suffered more than he, and that was the only thing that had held him back from the ultimate escape.

He had not returned in time for the end of the ball. He had walked around in the cold, welcoming the numbing sensation to fight his demons. He had been brought a message early this morning that his father desired to speak with him. He dressed and presented himself to the Duke as requested. He had been in England no more than a fortnight and mentally he felt as though he had fought the fiercest of battles. He knocked on the library door and entered.

"Did you take your cousin's innocence?" The Duke asked without any pretence or warning.

"Yes."

Silence.

"I see."

More silence.

"You should have told me."

Silence.

"You will offer for her at once."

"I do not think she…"

The Duke interrupted Nathaniel's protestations. "Lord Easton has been forced into announcing a betrothal between himself and Elinor, because last night your spiteful sister thought to ruin her." The Duke fought for composure. "I will not have Elinor saddled with the humiliation that will occur when Lord Easton finds out she is not pure. She will marry you, and we will prevent further disgrace."

Nathaniel was too stunned for words. He thought the last thing Elinor wished for was marriage to him, but he would offer if that would prevent her further harm.

"Beatrice will apologize and subdue the gossip, or she will find her world turned upside down. We will meet in the parlour in ten minutes," The Duke said with his usual finality, and turned away, his mind clearly made up.

Nathaniel walked out, dazed. Why had he come back? He never thought he would have to face Elinor, that's why. He was no longer afraid of hell, for it would be a reprieve for the existence he was living. He should have sent a letter to the Duke, explaining the whole of his sins, and shot himself on the battlefield to prevent shame to the family name. Instead, he had foolishly tried to redeem himself.

He made his way to the parlour and found Elinor. Seeing her raw fear of being alone with him made him even more remorseful, if that were possible. Everyone had joined them for that horrific family meeting, and his mother and sister had proceeded to sicken him further with their actions. Their treatment of Elinor, and their aspirations in life, represented everything he had come to abhor. Andrew had planted him a facer—the one act he understood.

The family had immediately removed to the country, barely on speaking terms with one another, all in their self-imposed misery. He must find a way to occupy himself there until the holidays were over, before he succumbed to madness. However, he refused to leave before attempting to make things better for Elinor. If she did not wish to marry Easton, he would do what he could to help, to somehow make up for all the destruction she had endured at his family's hands.

Nathaniel absented himself as much as possible from the household during the Christmas festivities. For six weeks, he was gone from sunup until sunset, running every horse in the stables to exhaustion. When he wasn't riding, he was walking along the cliffs in deep reverie, or fighting mills in the local taverns for sport. His nights were filled with restless sleep, despite his physical exhaustion, for he could not escape the horrors of his past.

Regardless of his father's interference and opinions, it appeared that Easton and Elinor truly wanted to wed each other. Seeing the two together at Christmas convinced Nathaniel. He resolved to remain in the country to see them marry. He felt they deserved his family's support after the trials they had suffered at the hands of the Loring clan, and then he would go back to London.

The day of the wedding finally arrived. Elinor had at last convinced the Duke that she truly desired to marry Easton, and so here they stood, watching her walk down the aisle. Her eyes met his. Elinor smiled at him—without fear. The look said everything that words could not, the one thing that could unburden his soul a fraction. He would never be free or absolved, but knowing she had obtained happiness was a weight lifted. Forgiveness was undeserved.

As soon as was polite, Nathaniel would escape from the wedding festivities. He stewed for a few more weeks until he could no longer tolerate it, and headed back to London.

Happy blessed birthday at last. Lady Lydia Markham was officially on the shelf and no longer under her uncle's thumb. Five-and-twenty, yet she felt much older most of the time. Her first order of business was to see her solicitor. She had plotted her escape since coming to the realization that Nathaniel did not want her, and she finally had enough money to remove to the Continent. Her mother was French and she spoke the language like a native. She had dreamt of a holiday cottage for years, but she would have to adjust her thoughts to being a widow. She had not had anyone she could depend upon for years, why not set forth on her own? She was so close to freedom she could almost taste it. The few happy memories she had of her parents were of times spent in such a place. She did not need much to manage, but she needed money to purchase a cottage. She began to have her maid sell off anything of value. She could sell her jewellery if necessary.

Lydia would have the solicitor set her up an account, and she would post off to Amelia as soon as she had met Nathaniel. She had not seen him in months. He had attended no society events since the ball. She had heard through servants' gossip that he spent his days boxing at Jackson's or out riding. She would just have to catch him on his way. She was quite determined. She rode in the carriage to the offices of Jonah E. Wheeler, Esq., wishing she could simply walk away and be done with men for good. She admitted her vanity had been hurt by Nathaniel's hasty dismissal of her, but she must swallow her pride and forge her own path.

Mr. Wheeler, a small squirrelly man, middle-aged in years, sat and listened to her wishes while he stroked his peppered beard.

"My dear Lady Lydia, I must object. It is not safe to move to the Continent without any family to guide you. What would foreigners do to help you, should you find yourself in need?"

What had her family here done to help her in her time of need?

"Sir, need I remind you that I have a five-year-old daughter to provide for? I wish to take her to live with me, now that I have reached my majority. I presume you see the difficulty in doing such a thing in England?"

Clearly embarrassed by her unashamed frankness, he sat quietly, and resumed stroking his beard in deep thought. "You would have to pass yourself off as a widow. Even in France they will be more accepting of you and your child that way."

"Of course."

"As your trusted advisor, having served your family for generations, I would be remiss in not recommending you appoint male trustees to advise you with your decisions."

She had to hold her tongue. Wise men such as her uncle, she assumed. "Thank you kindly for your advice, sir..." She smiled falsely and puffed up his consequence. "...but I trust you implicitly to advise me in all matters. I do not wish to make my daughter's existence known to anyone else."

He was somewhat pacified and not wholly immune to her charms, but was on the verge of apoplexy when she named Lord Fairmont as Amelia's guardian. She left a sealed note to be delivered to Lord Fairmont, should anything occur to her, God forbid, but she knew one look at Amelia and Nathaniel would not be able to refute his own child.

She took her leave, inwardly reeling at having to be dependent upon men such as Mr. Wheeler and her uncle, even more sure she was doing the right thing by removing to France. She had to find a way to speak with Nathaniel before she left. Time was running out. She thought about the past months. She had attended every possible ball, gala, soirée or dinner where she thought she might be able to find Nathaniel. She was usually more circumspect in her attendance, limiting herself to those events that were less particular about her reputation. She had endured the spiteful whispers of all the high and mighty in her desperate search to speak with him.

How dare she show her face here!
  That hussy is no better than she ought to be.
  Jezebel's daughter!

Many cut her directly. She smiled at their backs and kept walking with her head held high. She had long ago numbed herself to their condemnations. Her family's hypocritical treatment of her gave her little respect for those who held themselves above others.

Lydia became more frantic as she searched in vain for Nathaniel. She could not call on Beatrice, for it was rumoured she had been sent away for spreading malicious stories about her cousin. At last she became desperate enough to call on the Duchess, with the pretence of asking after Beatrice. Lydia was barely tolerated by the Duchess now, and only then because of her uncle's position in Society. When she arrived at Loring Place to leave her card, the knocker was removed from the front door and the shutters were closed. Of course, they had gone to Sussex. Her hopes sank.

She had become so consumed with her own plight, she had not realized she had even missed Christmas several weeks past. Her family never left for the country this time of year and spent little time together. The country would have been a blessing, for those were the few times she was able to see Amelia. She did not know how much longer she could maintain the façade. She had sold everything she could in order to finance her escape, but she needed more to survive. She was disgusted at the thought, but pleasing her uncle was the only way to earn enough money without walking the streets. She shuddered in repulsion, but had to put her daughter's welfare above her own. She was losing hope in Nathaniel as her saviour.

She left Loring Place disappointed, but decided to purchase a beautiful doll she had seen in a shop window. The smile on Amelia's face would be worth the shillings she'd had to part with, and she would do anything to make sure that smile never left her daughter's face. She picked up a trinket for Nurse as well, and made to return to Dannon House to compose a letter to send with the gifts, informing Nurse of her plans.

As Nathaniel rode up to the stables behind his home, he spotted Lady Lydia walking alone with her arms full. He left the horse with a groom and hurried to relieve her of her burden.

"Lady Lydia!" He called out to her to stop. He must have surprised her, for she nearly dropped her parcels. "Let me help you with that. Are you returning to Dannon House?" She nodded.

"Where is your maid?" He looked around.

She gave a slight shrug of the shoulders and only said, "These are not heavy, but thank you. How fortuitous; I have been needing to speak to you."

"Yes, you indicated as much at the ball."

They walked to the corner of Audley Street in silence. She had finally begun to speak when they were interrupted.

"My lord!" One of the Loring footmen ran up to him.

"Beg pardon, my lord," the footman said, out of breath. "But I was told this message was most urgent. Lord Uxbridge himself came to see you and asked me to see it personally into your hands. I was about to depart for Sussex to deliver it to you."

"Thank you, James. Will you please see Lady Lydia back to Dannon House?"

He turned back toward Lady Lydia. "Forgive me, but I must answer this at once."

"Of course," she answered quietly, but he was too distracted to notice, already walking away.

He made haste to change into his regimentals and set out immediately for the Earl's residence, hopeful that his fellow Hussars would provide some diversion. He arrived in Burlington Street and was ushered immediately into the Earl's sanctum. There he was surrounded by several fellow cavalrymen in preparations for deployment.

At his being announced, several junior officers snapped to attention.

"Sir," Nathaniel said, saluting the general.

"Ah, Fairmont. As you can see we are preparing to set out."

"What's this? More occupation?" Nathaniel asked in notable confusion.

"Ah. You have not yet heard. Boney has made his escape from Elba. We are to set out immediately." Uxbridge looked around his desk.

"Lieutenant, find me the dispatch." A young, fresh-faced officer found the errant missive and handed it to the Earl. "Best read it for yourself. From the Duke."

Nathaniel scanned the familiar scrawl in astonishment. He was to lead one of the Life Guard regiments to the Continent and report to Lord Somerset, head of the Household Brigade, in Brussels with all urgency. Lord Uxbridge would be the head of all cavalry.

"A Household Regiment." Nathaniel tasted the words, uncertain how he felt about exchanging his blue tunic for a red one, having been a hussar for the past six years.

"A cheeser, sir!" one of the officers teased.

"Surely he only jests!" Nathaniel exclaimed.

"I think not. Crusty he may be, but never let him be accused of being a fool. These boys are fairly green in action, and will require all of our effort to present them admirably in the trenches. I beg of you, refrain from telling them how abominably dirty they will become on the field."

Ruptures of laughter filled the room. The Life Guards were considered the dandy set of the cavalry, the elite. The hussars and infantry took much pride in razzing them.

Nathaniel could not help but remark, "Sir, you have proven there is hope for all Tulips."

"Touché, Fairmont," Lord Uxbridge said, flashing his famous smile. He was said to be the most dashing beau ever to wear the hussar uniform. "One cannot fault a man for wanting to wear the uniform well. Will Loring be a problem?"

"I will speak with him directly. I do not believe it to be a hopeless case."

"Very well. Send word as soon as possible. I plan to set forth within the fortnight. As you know, our forces are greatly depleted and we need every man of experience we can gather."

Nathaniel nodded, saluted, and departed.

Nathaniel dreaded the talk with his father, for he knew the Duke could pull the strings to prevent his joining the fight against Napoleon. He had to impart his desire to return without offending his father's sense of pride. His parents had just returned to London after the Duke had sent his sister Beatrice to Scotland. He strolled into a discussion of his sister's banishment to obscurity, his parents at odds about her handling, as usual. His mother was summarily dismissed. His father turned and focused on him.

"How are you adjusting to England, my son? I have not seen much of you," the Duke enquired.

"I confess, I would rather be elsewhere. I feel decidedly out of place."

"Nonsense! Whatever put such a notion in your head?" The Duke looked up questioningly.

"I am a soldier; fighting is in my blood now. Wellington sent word that Napoleon has escaped and has requested my return, with your permission of course. With so many of our forces depleted with the American War, he is lacking for experience to mount a campaign against Boney."

"I see." This was not what the Duke wanted to hear, by the look on his face.

"I cannot attend social functions gaily, knowing there is a war going on while my fellow soldiers fight for our freedom. I do not fit into Society any longer. I know Elinor has forgiven me, but if it pains me every time I see her, I can only imagine how she feels. She is content with Easton and deserves to be happy."

"But you have a duty as my heir! To the people here!" the Duke said in exasperation.

Nathaniel shook his head. "I know this is difficult for you to understand, Father. Andrew is more than capable of helping, should you need it, and you are hardly in your dotage."

"It is not right."

"Perhaps when Boney is defeated I will feel differently, but being here reminds me of everything I did wrong that I cannot make right. The wounds are still too fresh."

The Duke sat in silence. "I do not agree, but I will truly not have you here if your heart is there."

"Thank you, Father." The Duke stood to embrace Nathaniel, and tears gathered in his eyes.

Nathaniel escaped to Gentleman Jackson's boxing saloon. Since spirits were not an option, he frequented the joint to soothe his anxieties in the form of fisticuffs. He was able to engage the gentleman himself and his cousin Andrew that morning.

The exercise helped him to clear his head. He'd had second thoughts after seeing Lydia and his father. But after talking things over with Andrew, he left knowing he was doing the right thing. Andrew would help take care of his family should anything happen to him.

Dearest Nurse,

I wish I could have been with you for Christmas. I hope these gifts bring smiles.

I am pleased to say I shall be joining you shortly. I am finally able to say with confidence we will all be together again soon—for good.

Start packing for France!

Au Revoir,

Lydia

Lydia sealed her somewhat cryptic note to her nurse. Her maid would help her see that the package was delivered.

After her errand, Lydia decided to venture home through the park on the early spring day. She was elated. She had not felt such freedom, nor anticipation for her future since the summer Nathaniel had wooed her. She came upon many of her old court, all eager to spread the news. Bonaparte had escaped Elba, and Lord Uxbridge and Lord Fairmont had posted with the Household Guard to Brussels.

No! He had left her again. Lydia could not breathe; her vision blurred. Had it not been for the lively discussion that ensued, diverting her attention, she might have succumbed to a swoon—or a loud scream. There was a fashionable exodus to Brussels of those eager to be near the action; there was already a portion of Society following the Guards there in occupation, she knew. Her mind immediately began to swirl with the possibilities. France was no longer a safe option. Lydia was nothing if not resourceful; it was certainly a diversion in her plan, but it would be easier to find Nathaniel in Brussels amongst the soldiers and away from the *ton's* prying eyes.

Lydia excused herself and returned to Dannon House to pack. She had not planned on the added time or expense of a foray to Brussels. She had little choice but to sell what remained of her jewels. She sent a note to her solicitor to arrange the sale of the gems, and also her transport to Wiltshire. Oh, the freedoms of reaching one's majority! She was, however, unsure how to achieve this new goal. First, she must get herself to Wiltshire, then she would decide how best to convince Nurse to go to Brussels instead.

The solicitor had done her bidding. Lydia had been unsure of his willingness to comply with her unusual requests. Lydia held a purse from selling everything she had and passage in her hands for her transport to Wiltshire, and from there, passage for three to the Continent via Portsmouth. This had been most difficult to obtain at this time, Mr. Wheeler explained in his note, with all of the soldiers and supplies being transported. Civilians were limited to the Port of Dieppe for arrival. He could be of no service with accommodation in Brussels at such short notice. Lydia felt sure something could be found once they arrived and put this from the back of her mind. Her greater concern was making her escape from her uncle's house unnoticed.

She had begun to take belongings to the garden discreetly, to a trunk. She had few possessions left after selling everything of value, but some things could not be parted with. The chaise was to take her up in the back alley, where it would be possible to load her trunk without notice.

She stood at the door to her room ready to open it for the last time and leave, she prayed. As she reached for the handle, she saw it turn before her and froze. She stood wide-eyed in horror, then quickly shoved the last small bag of her belongings under a chair. Her uncle peeped his head around the door and saw her.

"Ah, good, you are still awake. I was afraid I missed your birthday."

"No, sir, you are still in time." She feigned her best smile.

"I brought you something I think you will be pleased with." He held out a gift that could only be one thing.

Lydia teetered. She would love nothing more than to shove the box down his disgusting throat. But, by the size of it, she might be able to purchase the small cottage and her freedom. She glanced at the clock. She only had a short time until the coach would arrive.

"Go on, open it." Her uncle was clearly proud of his generous gift to her.

She has hesitated, then lifted the lid and beheld an astonishing necklace of large diamond stones. "Sir, I am not sure what to say."

"Lydia, dearest, surely you know by now that words are not what I'm looking for. You have been a most obliging girl, and I wanted to reward your good behaviour."

The familiar taste of bile rose in her throat. She nodded and allowed her uncle to do his worst. One last time. For their future.

After the hallway was clear, she grabbed her cloak, bag and the necklace and hurried down to the garden, desperately hoping the coach had not left. Her maid had been good enough to see the trunk loaded and held the coach for her. Meggie gave her a knowing look. Lydia hugged her tightly; the woman had been the only one who had supported her in this forsaken house. She struggled to contain her emotion.

"I wish you could come along," she said sadly.

There were no more words to say; this had been discussed. She climbed in the coach. There was no time to waste. The door was closed and the horses given their heads.

It was morning by the time Lydia arrived at her nurse's small cottage. She was nervous every time she came to see Amelia, for fear that she would have forgotten her. Nurse opened the door and gave a shout of happiness. She held her arms open and Lydia gladly fell into them. After a much-needed embrace from the only person Lydia had ever received affection from, save that brief interlude with Nathaniel, she immediately enquired after Amelia.

"She's over at the vicarage learning her letters. She will be back soon."

Lydia did not wish to wait one more moment to see her beloved daughter, but it would give her a chance to speak to Nurse with privacy and put herself to rights.

After being refreshed with hot scones and a fresh cup of tea, she poured the entirety of her situation and her plan into poor old Nurse's ears.

CHAPTER 7

*R*elief did not adequately describe Nathaniel's feelings the moment he stepped on the boat. He watched England fade away across the Channel with a mix of emotions. He was not certain he would ever return. He felt he did more harm than good by being present on the island. Until he was convinced otherwise, he would not set foot ashore there again. For now, defeating Bonaparte was of the utmost consideration. He was sceptical of leading the Hyde Park Soldiers, most on their first foray against the wily Corsican general, but their horsemanship would be welcome if they could overcome their fear of dirtying their impeccable uniforms. He laughed. He could not resist the barb, even in his thoughts.

He tried not to cringe as he looked his own new scarlet tunic over. He felt certain he would make a better target in red. He preferred the unadorned field uniform to the decorated dress uniform favoured by the Life Guards. None of the ostentation would matter in the heat of the battle, he reflected. Every soldier bled and died the same. The great equalizer.

Ostend came into view; he had best accept his place in his regiment or he could not expect unity from his men. He had to laugh at himself for his reversed prejudice. Most would assume a duke's heir fit for nothing more than palace guard with pomp and circumstance, yet he was not suited for such goings-on. Many of the best soldiers were great peers. But he knew these fellows were in for an initiation which would change their lives forever, and there was no going back. He thought back to his own lack of training when he had been thrust into army life and ill-equipped for battle. He had forged ahead and survived. On further reflection, there really was very little to fully prepare one for battle. Skill with a sabre and horse were required, but much more relied on intuition and fate. Confidence in a leader to begin the fight was essential, however, so he let go once again of Lord Fairmont, and placed the battle-hardened Colonel Fairmont firmly in place.

"Red becomes you, Fairmont!" a voice from behind said good-humouredly.

"Would it be impertinent to tell you to stubble it, sir?" Nathaniel laughed. "Were it anyone other than you, I might have planted them a facer."

"I meant it as the highest compliment, I'm sure," Lord Uxbridge said sardonically.

"I would myself enjoy seeing you sport the scarlet."

Uxbridge shuddered dramatically. "I would have been forced to resign immediately!"

"Nothing short of an elopement would have prevailed upon you to miss this fight!"

"You put me to the blush, Fairmont!"

"I thought you incapable...sir!" Nathaniel added at the last moment with a laugh.

"So true," Uxbridge said with a twinkle in his eye. He had a scandalous reputation after having run off with Wellington's married sister, but there were few that compared to his skill as a general when it came to war and Wellington would take the best man on the battlefield.

The two stared out over the water as a sandy beach came nearer into view. When Uxbridge spoke again, it was in a different tone.

"Are you prepared to rally these greenhorns? I must say, I think it a brilliant move on Hookey's part."

"Thank you, sir. I trust your confidence will not be misplaced."

"Where you lead, they will follow. I, as well as Somerset, will be counting on you to keep them intent and fighting. But I need not tell you this," he said, waving his hand through the air.

"Your words are not ill-judged. I was only now chastising myself over my reluctance. However, that will do no more than lower morale and spirits and cause rancour amongst the men. I collect I can rely on their superior breeding and horsemanship to not fail their country," Nathaniel said thoughtfully.

"Just so, Fairmont. Just so," Uxbridge said in agreement.

The Guards were restless from their crossing, and the horses were eager to be on land. All were too anxious to mount up and proceed to their appointed quarters at Liederkerke, delighted to be in the fight at last. The journey began, and Nathaniel set out to rally his men.

Once settled in camp, Nathaniel embarked upon his task to bond with his new regiment. He knew personally of Napoleon's prowess, and word was that time before battle was short. He had never before considered how to go about this task, as training and fighting together naturally united people. His Hussars would have followed him anywhere, knowing he would be right alongside them. He had neither the luxury of time, nor more than minuscule acquaintance with many of these pups, since they were in short coats when he'd left for the Peninsula. They, however, held him in something akin to awe as the Duke of Loring's heir and with a reputation as a fierce warrior and cavalryman. Would that it were enough to carry them through when in the heat of battle.

The first official act as leader of the 1st Life Guards was to present in formation at a review of British troops to be held on the banks of the Dender, Lord Somerset leading the full Household Brigade. Once in place, they awaited the arrival of the Commander and his entourage to survey his army. The day was sweltering in full uniform, and they spent hours in the scorching sun before that familiar hooked nose and cocked hat arrived along with the other leaders of the Allied Army and they presented themselves.

Slowly, the various commanders passed by as they all held themselves at rigid attention, meeting with glowing approval. The Duke, a man of few words, but of hawkish notice, stopped short when he reached Nathaniel's regiment.

"Where is Abbott? Did he not journey with you?"

"No, my lord. There was no summons included in the missive to myself."

Wellington glanced toward Uxbridge, who nodded agreement. Wellington looked toward the nearest aide-de-camp and said, "See to it at once! How can Abbott think I mean to go on without him?"

Not expecting a reply, he moved forward, shaking his head in consternation for this oversight.

∾

"You want to do what, Lydia Abigail Markham?" Nurse's eyes were as wide as saucers.

"I want us all to remove to Brussels until it is safe to move on to France," Lydia pronounced.

"In the middle of a war? Have you lost your mind?" Nurse exclaimed.

"I have been assured that Brussels is safe, and all will be over soon. As soon as Wellington defeats Bonaparte, we may advance to the south," Lydia said as convincingly as she could.

"I am too old for this, Lady Lydia. This old bag of bones cannot handle that much adventure." Nurse shook her head.

"Nonsense! You must come with me. I will need your help, I am sure. Besides, Amelia will miss you and may not be completely comfortable with me." Lydia looked away as she said this, still ashamed of her lack of presence in Amelia's life, and her lack of motherly skills. A thought occurred to her. "Unless...have you someone here you wish to stay for?"

Nurse flushed red and denied the accusation vehemently. "Of course I do not have a beau!"

"Then why are you so opposed to the notion? You know I cannot stay here. It will not take my uncle long to discover I am gone. He may not care in the least, but..." It was better left unspoken.

Nurse let out a loud sigh of exasperation. Her eyes narrowed. "That other limb of Satan will be there, won't he?" The first limb referred to her uncle.

Lydia rose to Nathaniel's defence. "He still does not know! I did not get a chance to tell him! I only wish to let him know about Amelia."

Nurse let out a sceptical *humph*. "But you did see him?"

Lydia nodded. She turned away so Nurse would not see her tears. She told herself it was for Amelia's sake. She was determined to keep her heart unaffected.

"I am sorry, my dear. But, I cannot see how you expect to find him amongst thousands of soldiers in a large foreign city. What makes you think he will care one way or the other if you do tell him?"

"I am not certain, Nurse. But I cannot bear that he does not know. For Amelia's sake I must try."

Nurse could never resist her big pleading blue eyes, she knew.

"I am sure I am going to regret this."

"Oh, Nurse! Thank you!"

As Lydia was hugging Nurse, a small, angelic voice said from the doorway, "Mama?"

"Oh, my love, come here and give Mama a hug! I have missed you so!" Lydia bent down to gather her petite little girl in her arms.

She was rewarded with a fierce squeeze—as hard as a two-stone five-year-old child could muster.

"Why are you cwying, Mama?"

"Because I am happy to see you!" Lydia said with a smile. She dared not say she was happy to be remembered.

The little face wrinkled in thought. "You cwy when you are happy?"

"Sometimes, my love. I am also excited, for we are to go on an adventure."

Big grey eyes widened and sparkled with excitement. "An adventure?"

"Oh, yes! Let us talk about it over luncheon." The little girl clung to her mama, obviously afraid she would have to leave again. Lydia was more than happy to allow this luxury. Nurse was suspiciously silent as she laid out the victuals, wiping her eyes from time to time.

Lord Dannon awoke the next morning, feeling as if he would like more of what he had partaken of the night before with his lovely niece. He ought to receive plenty of benefit from that diamond trinket. He certainly did not mind parting with a small fortune to keep the mistress within his own walls happy. Women were so predictable.

He tapped lightly on Lydia's door, smiling about his brilliant birthday gift to her. It had been too dark to see her appreciative gleam last night. This morning he would insist she wear nothing but the necklace. Perhaps she would finally cease acting the prude. He knocked again impatiently, but with no answer; she was still asleep. He must have worn her out last night, he thought lasciviously. He chuckled. He would enjoy waking her and he knew just how to do it. He gently opened the door. The curtains were still drawn. He crept over to the bed and pulled back its curtains.

His excitement turned to anger when he saw the empty bed, and that it was undisturbed, save for the evidence of their tryst. He stomped over to the window and thrust back the curtains. He checked her drawers and her dressing room—his fears were confirmed. All of her belongings had been removed. Lydia was gone.

He punched the looking-glass and it shattered. How dare the little trollop run away! She had nothing to survive on but a pittance—and his diamond necklace. No, she was not so stupid as that. He paced around the room furiously, trying to think of where she might have run off to. The only person she could have run off to was…Fairmont.

He could not have her! She belonged to him. She owed him. He vowed to track her to the ends of the earth, if that was what was necessary.

He ran down the stairs and into his study, shouting frantically for his butler, with no regard for his state of undress.

"Send to Bow Street immediately, Cummins!" He paced the room with fury.

The stoic butler replied, "Yes, my lord. What shall I say is the matter, my lord?"

"Lady Lydia is missing and she must be found." He stormed over to the decanter and poured a large serving of whisky, downing it in one swallow.

"Very good, my lord." The butler bowed, unperturbed. "Shall I send for the doctor to tend to your hand?" He indicated the blood dripping down his employer's arm, from when he'd shattered the glass.

Lord Dannon looked down in surprise and shrugged. "It is nothing."

CHAPTER 8

The glamour of the grand adventure was over with quickly. They had escaped detection by her wicked uncle, but being obliged to economize meant taking the stage to Portsmouth and no private cabin on the ship. Lydia could have borne this herself with no great pains, but having a child succumb to motion sickness amongst a crowd of strangers was not making for a pleasant journey. The crossing was extremely rough, and therefore never-ending, and there was no room at the inns once they arrived in Dieppe. The threesome was obliged to ride in the back of a donkey cart until they found a farmhouse with a spare room for accommodation.

"A mighty fine fix we are in, Lady Lydia." Nurse grumbled.

"You just remember the first limb of Satan, Nurse, and that makes this more bearable."

A weary little Amelia popped her head from her nurse's shoulder, "What is a lamb of Satan, Mama?"

"Never you mind that, child," Nurse said with a meaningful look toward Lydia. "What plans do you have from here?"

"Only to get to Brussels, however we may. I will speak to the owner of this accommodation and see if he knows how to arrange passage. I heard on the boat that it is still over two hundred miles from here."

"Oh, heavens." Nurse crossed herself. "It might be best to take our chances in the south, Lady Lydia."

"You know why we cannot do that! I own, circumstances are not close to ideal."

Nurse snorted. Lydia continued, "But there is still the chance *someone* might be willing to help us in our plight."

"And what happens when that *someone* sends you on your way?"

"I confess I am not sure. I might have to introduce him to her." Lydia glanced over at her beautiful child playing with a litter of kittens in the corner. "He cannot deny her."

"No, but there is no saying he will do what's right by her. Or you." Nurse sniffed and shook her head.

"I care not for me."

"Fustian!" Nurse did not believe Lydia's words.

The mistress of the farmhouse entered with a tray of cold meat and bread, interrupting them.

"*Merci, madame. Nous sommes très reconnaissants pour votre hospitalité.*" Lydia greeted the woman in her native tongue.

The woman looked surprised at the fluency of her visitor's French. Perhaps she wasn't sure if they were foreigners. She seemed to warm to them immediately, and went into raptures over the vision of an angel that was Amelia. "*Belle ange doré!*"

Once deciding that a respectable-looking widow with a nurse and a beautiful child meant no harm, the woman was willing to help with anything asked. Lydia proceeded to find herself on excellent terms with her, and was able to arrange transportation to the next town when the woman's husband drove the produce to market. He would help them find decent lodgings there.

Lydia was proud that something had finally gone in their favour, and Nurse's grumblings were quieter for the remainder of the night.

Three days they were obliged to wait before the farmer went to market; three days for Amelia to become inseparable from one of the kittens. One more passenger was added to their ménage, and Lydia was certain that her hands and ankles would be scratched for the remainder of the cat's life. But the kitten did not bite or scratch at Amelia, and it kept her entertained, therefore Lydia decided to let it come.

An old chicken cart was not what Lydia had in mind when she had arranged a lift, but there was no telling when another mode of travel would be available to them. Luxury was the furthest thing from her mind. Nurse and Amelia were riding on the box with the farmer, and Lydia was forced to ride in the back of the cart with live chickens and any number of potatoes, carrots and cabbages that were being taken to market in Abbeville. Fifty miles she was obliged to ride in such a fashion. The old dirt roads were deeply rutted from the spring rains, and there being no cushion from the iron wheels, it made for quite a beating that Lydia received on this stage of the journey. She refused to utter one word of complaint, or Nurse would ring a peal over her, though she was not sure she would be able to move for a few days after sitting in such cramped quarters.

They passed through some beautiful countryside, not too far from where she hoped to find a cottage when the war was over. She did her best to take notice of the beautiful rivers, rolling hills and vineyards, instead of the pungent smell of the chicken cart and the strong stink of manure from the farms when the winds blew in their direction. The farmer only laughed when Amelia would dramatically pinch her nose and exclaim, "Eeeeewwww!"

The farmer was as good as his word, and saw them placed in small but clean lodgings. The French were obliging to a native speaker who paid her shot, but the journey on to Brussels took a week more to accomplish with severe trials on Nurse's nerves and Lydia's ingenuity. It was difficult to travel with a small child in the best of circumstances, therefore the journey felt painfully long. Lydia was discovering a five-year-old child was a never-ending source of chatter and curiosity. If Amelia grew quiet, she knew she was sleeping!

Lydia felt sure Nurse would refuse to go one foot further when the only mode of transportation she could find was on the back of donkeys. Nurse was terrified of riding animals, but they were slow moving and she did not have to ride for too long.

Thus, Lydia's grand entrance into the Grand Place in Brussels was made. At several points along the way, she doubted if they would ever make it. She had not counted on the difficulties of finding transport or the length of time it would take to reach the city. The town was buzzing with the news of the French marching at any moment. Every inn was crowded with soldiers, but Lydia was finally able to secure a small house on the Rue de la Madelaine from a family evacuating due to the threat of war.

Lydia began the search for Nathaniel. She knew not the name of his regiment. Discreet enquiry informed her that he was no longer wearing the blue of the Hussars. She had not foreseen the difficulty of locating him once in Brussels, but soon discovered over twelve thousand troops were in the vicinity. Undaunted, she pressed onward despite weeks wasted in her search. She had not come this far only to give up so easily.

She was surprised at the amount of English Society present, and began to feel she might have need to mingle with some of them in order to obtain the desired information. She had hoped to maintain a modicum of invisibility, fearing word might reach her uncle. Though she had travelled with her nurse, she was unable to go about the town accompanied by her unknown daughter, and was careful to attract no notice when she did venture out alone. Nurse had taken Amelia to the park when Lydia returned from another fruitless search for Nathaniel's whereabouts. She decided to join them on the sunny late spring day.

She strolled distractedly toward the park, desperately searching her mind for options open to her while trying to maintain anonymity. She rounded the corner onto the Rue Royale and ran straight into Major Andrew Abbott.

"I beg your pardon, sir!" Lydia said in English, noticing the scarlet uniform of her country.

"Lady Lydia?" Andrew said with surprise, and made a quick bow.

"Major Abbott." She dropped a brief curtsy.

"I did not know you were in Brussels. What brings you here? Following the drum?" he teased.

"Not precisely. I prefer it not be made known that I am here."

"Of course. Can I be of assistance?"

Lydia hesitated. Major Abbott was cousin to Nathaniel, and he might be able to relieve her search at once. It was worth the risk. "Would you happen to know where I might find Lord Fairmont?"

Astonishment crossed Andrew's face. "I have only now arrived, but I can contrive to find out shortly."

"Would you be so kind as to let me know so that a message may be given to him?"

"I suppose that could be arranged. Is there something I might help you with? Brussels is a long way to come to deliver a message."

Emotion crossed Lydia's face. Andrew must have seen enough to concern him. "I will get word to Fairmont. Might I have your direction if he is able to get away?"

Lydia nodded and proceeded to inform Andrew of the house she had rented not far from the park. "The small white stone house with a red door and red shutters."

"I am at Wellington's headquarters, should you need anything, Lady Lydia. I will send word to Fairmont immediately." He pointed down the street toward Wellington's lodgings.

"I am ever so grateful, Major Abbott. I was beginning to despair of finding him."

Andrew bowed. "I am happy to be of service."

Lydia watched Major Abbott walk away. Her pulse was racing with nervousness. She prayed she was not on a fool's errand.

"Lydia is in Brussels?" Nathaniel questioned with disbelief.

"Aye. She seemed desperate to speak to you," Andrew replied.

"She mentioned as much in London. Other events distracted me, and I was unable to call on her before I returned here."

"She also asked me to keep her presence here quiet."

"Whatever could be the matter? I cannot imagine anything urgent enough to bring her here." Nathaniel was utterly perplexed.

"I know not, but she seemed most determined to find you."

"I had better set out directly. Are you returning now?"

"Yes. I only came to see you. I felt it best to deliver this message in person. I know you had some understanding with her in the past."

"Yes." Nathaniel kept looking straight ahead.

"Lady Lydia has developed a bit of a..." Andrew hesitated, "...reputation over the years."

"I understand. I know she was much in my sister's company." That explained much, but disturbed his conscience further. "Thank you for coming yourself. Let me speak with Somerset and tell him of my errand, and I will set off with you directly."

The two rode hard for the better part of the fifteen-mile trip. Nathaniel could not form any coherent conclusions about why Lydia could desire speech with him. Andrew parted with him to return to headquarters, and Nathaniel made his way to the small house with the red door where Lydia was said to be.

Several hours had passed since Lydia had left Major Abbott on the Rue Royale. She had no idea how long it would be until Nathaniel received her message, nor whether he would be able to present himself to her. They had only just finished supper and Nurse had whisked Amelia off for her bath when a knock sounded upon the door. Lydia opened the door herself to find Nathaniel upon the step.

Unable to hide her emotion, she declared, "Oh, thank God you have come!" She pulled him inside and led him to the small sitting room.

"Whatever has happened, Lydia? What has brought you to Brussels?"

Lydia had rehearsed the speech she would give him over and over in her mind for years. She had hoped that she would be able to be on better terms with Nathaniel before breaking the news to him, but no such luxury existed in her mind any longer. Now that the moment was before her, all eloquency of speech absented itself and she blurted out her news.

"We have a daughter."

Nathaniel stood still for several moments before walking over to the mantel. Perhaps he did not believe her. She waited in silence, watching him absorb this unforeseen news. He finally turned to look at her. "Why am I only now hearing of this? She must be several years old by now!" he said angrily.

"She is five."

"I do not understand. Could you not have sent word?" He was upset.

She flushed. Lydia tried to compose her thoughts. She did not wish to go into the circumstances that surrounded her decisions at the time when she had found herself single, increasing, abandoned, and threatened by her uncle. She bit her lip to stop the tremble that threatened to betray her emotions.

Nathaniel seemed to realize some of these things as he processed this revelation. In a calmer voice he said, "Forgive me, Lydia. I am only in shock. I imagine the situation was not easy to deal with on your own."

Lydia had to turn away to hide her shame.

"What has become of our... our daughter?" Nathaniel asked slowly, as if tasting the feel of the new word.

"That is why I have sought you out. I only reached my majority recently, and obtained freedom from my guardian." She turned toward him again. If Nathaniel thought her choice of words odd, he did not betray it on his face.

She continued, "I have been able to keep Amelia hidden with my old nurse for all these years. I have been saving what I was able in order to purchase a cottage in France. I intend to set myself up as a widow and raise her free from the...*stigma*, but I am afraid I was unable to save enough. That is why I seek your help."

"Nonsense!"

"Pardon?" Had she heard him correctly?

"You will do no such thing!" He was becoming angry again.

"I will not raise my daughter as a bastard in the *ton's* eyes!" she protested indignantly. She had not endured more than six years of hell to have it all undone.

"Why did you not seek help from my father or your uncle?"

"Ha! My uncle? I am fortunate I was able to save our daughter from his clutches. He used me as an excuse to entertain himself. He was to have sent her to the foundling home! And as for your father, do you believe he would have brought you home to marry me?"

"He might have at least supported you," Nathaniel said quietly.

"I have managed. I had hoped to speak with you on the matter in London, but knowing you had departed firmed my resolve to escape my uncle and seek your help. If you find you are unable to do so, we will continue on after the fighting and make do as best we may," she said proudly, with a lift to her chin.

"We?"

"Nurse and Amelia are with me."

"She is with you?"

Lydia nodded. She should not have told him that yet.

"May I see her?" he asked with a plea in his voice.

"I am not certain that is a good idea."

"Lydia, I will see my daughter. You cannot expect me to abandon her!"

"I was not sure at all what I expected."

"Please." Nathaniel pleaded quietly with those same eyes of his daughter's.

She paused to think, and realized it was useless to resist. "Very well. Let me see if she is finished with her bath." Lydia left and returned a few minutes later with Nathaniel's butter stamp. The angelic, petite version of himself rendered Nathaniel speechless.

"This is Amelia." Lydia brought the child forward.

"How do you do, sir." Amelia made a curtsy to Nathaniel. "Who are you?"

Nathaniel, tears in his eyes, said, "I am your papa."

CHAPTER 9

I always wanted to have a papa! Mama said mine was a soldier away at the war." Amelia crawled up onto his lap, and began to play with his buttons.

"Yes, I have been away. I am sorry we are only now meeting." Nathaniel reached up to stroke one of her golden curls, touching to see if she was real, coming to terms with his child.

"It's all right, Papa. I know you have been busy."

"Thank you, that is kind of you," he said, amused at her open manners and easy forgiveness.

"Will you come back to play with me soon? I had to leave all of my fwiends in England."

"I would be honoured, Amelia."

She reached up and kissed him on the cheek.

"Can I have a pony? I have always wanted a pony."

"Amelia!" Lydia chastised the child for her poor manners.

"Who can she ask for such things, if not her papa?" Nathaniel asked. For this he was rewarded with another kiss. He chuckled. "I wonder where she gets her charm from?" he asked rhetorically as he tweaked her on the nose.

Nurse entered the room and curtsied to Nathaniel. "Off to bed with you, little miss."

"But I just met my papa!" Amelia protested.

"I will be back soon, I promise." Amelia clung to Nathaniel's neck, refusing to let go.

"Must you go?" Her eyes filled with tears and her bottom lip started to quiver.

"I have to return to my regiment, but I will visit as soon as I can."

Nurse came over and tried to peel Amelia from him. He looked over the girl's head at Nurse and shook his head.

"How about I tell you a bedtime story and tuck you in?" he suggested.

She nodded her head without loosening her hold.

"Wait!" Amelia looked up and shouted.

"What is it, my dear?" Nathaniel asked worriedly.

"We must not leave *Chaton*!"

"Ah, silly Papa. How could I forget *Chaton*?" He scooped up the kitten, and then carried them to the bed. He lay down beside Amelia on her bed, and placed the kitten beside her.

"What story would you like to hear?"

"Cindewella!"

"Of course. Let us see if my memory serves me. This story is rather new to me. There once lived a rich man whose wife became ill. She called her only daughter to her bedside..."

Nathaniel proceeded to muddle his way through the story. Amelia kept touching his face and his arms, snuggling close. He found his heart being surrounded and squeezed by five-year-old fingers, placing an eternal hold on him. Her eyes became heavy, but would pop open while a little voice corrected her papa when he stumbled over any part of the tale. She fell asleep in his arms, and he reluctantly rose, kissed her head and tucked her blankets up under her chin.

Lydia watched this touching scene; her lost love being so tender with his daughter caused her heart to ache in her chest. They tiptoed from the room, and Nathaniel made to leave.

"I will return as soon as I am able." He hesitated, choosing his words carefully. "Word is the French are marching upon us soon, but I do not know when that will take place. I need time to think through everything."

Lydia nodded. She understood his sentiments.

He took her hand and gave it a gentle squeeze before leaving. "Thank you for finding me."

Lydia closed the door behind him, then slid down the door, slumping over into deep sobs.

Nathaniel mounted his horse, but instead of hurrying back to camp, he trotted slowly, needing time to adjust to the complete reversal in his life. *I am a father.* He could not stop thinking the words. *I have a daughter.* The reality of it all changed his perspective. Was this a second chance for his soul? One look and he had been lost to those big grey eyes, long golden curls and a smile to warm his ice-cold heart. He had not thought that possible. An enchanting little thing, she was, his Amelia. Her personality—as bold as you please—was the most captivating thing about her. He laughed out loud.

Suddenly, his life took on a whole new meaning. How had Lydia come to this pass? Why had she not sent word? He shook his head. There was no point in questioning her choices in the past. Lydia, to her credit, had found a way to manage without his help, and their daughter seemed none the worse for it. He now understood the pain he had seen in Lydia's eyes in London. She had not been pining after him for all of these years, she had been surviving. It could not have been easy.

Lydia had not expected Nathaniel to react so calmly or warmly to his child. She had expected him to be defensive and demand proof. How much harder it would be to leave him again, but leave she must. She did not wish to follow the drum with a small child, even should he offer. What would be the point now after so many years? She no longer cared if she married. Nathaniel no longer loved her. Had he returned to London with the same affection, she would have run to him with open arms. She had seen nothing of love in his eyes or his demeanour. Now, she only wanted her child provided for.

The thought of a one-sided marriage was detestable to her now that she had choices. She had lived through such a marriage with her aunt and uncle. She had tried to find a marriage of convenience, as her only option to escape her uncle, for many years. But now she was free, and loveless marriages only brought resentment. She would have all the affection she needed from Amelia.

With those decisions made, she drifted off into a restless sleep, at least hopeful that Nathaniel would provide for their daughter.

"We shall marry at once." Nathaniel strolled into the parlour the next morning with this proclamation. "I obtained only enough leave to settle these matters, but then I must return quickly." He paced around the room as if in a hurry.

"We will do no such thing!" Lydia was indignant. She would not be commanded like one of his troops.

He halted. "I beg your pardon?"

"I do not wish to marry you." Not when he did not want her as well.

"You wish to label our child a bastard?" he asked angrily.

"Of course not! I have worked hard to prevent that. I told you my wishes."

"Ah. To set yourself up as a respectable widow in France. I can stop you, if I must. It would take little effort to prove her my daughter."

Lydia knew this to be true. Not only was Nathaniel's father a powerful duke, Amelia looked just like him.

"You would take her from me?" she asked, fearing his answer.

"That is exactly what you propose! Did it not occur to you that I would wish to be a part of her life?" He was incredulous.

"Actually, no. When I received your letter six years ago, I assumed you had washed your hands of me. Were I not desperate to provide for her until I come into my full inheritance, I should not have bothered you now!"

"What a monster you must think me. I might not have been able to return on the next ship, but I would have taken care of you both!" He looked away. "I had to go. I did not want to leave you."

Tears streamed from Lydia's eyes. She had been so young and unsure of what to do. Her uncle had threatened her with his heavy hand, and she'd had little choice. Nathaniel's words stripped away her last piece of armour. He pulled her into his arms and she wept. When her tears ran no more, Nathaniel pulled back to look at her face.

"Would it be horrible to be married to me? I could likely die in battle, and at least you would be provided for, with my name to protect you."

"Please do not speak of such things. I could not bear that."

"So you have a small amount of affection left for me?" he coaxed.

"You wretch." The corner of her mouth gave the hint of a smile despite herself.

"We loved each other in earnest once. Our child was conceived in love."

"I was only your calf-love," she protested half-heartedly.

"Lydia, I can honestly say I have loved no other. True, I have devoted myself to the army, but I will sell out after this campaign and do my best to see you both happy."

"What about Elinor?" He'd had relations with her as well, unless Beatrice had been merely gossiping.

Nathaniel hesitated before speaking. "I made a mistake." He swallowed with difficulty. "A horrid mistake."

Lydia suppressed a gasp. She never would have thought Nathaniel capable of such behaviour. That was nothing like the man she knew.

"That is why I left so suddenly. Had I known I was abandoning you in such a way, I would have fought my father to stay. I did not think myself worthy of you any more." Nathaniel choked back tears before speaking again. "Amelia makes me want to live again, to be a better man. Please do not take her from me."

Lydia hesitated. He was in earnest. She was hardly without sin herself, and she could not bear to live without Amelia. She looked down.

"I suppose we should try, for Amelia's sake."

Nathaniel left the house dumbfounded. Lydia's reaction confused him. Why would she not want to legitimize Amelia? If her refusal had come after his confession about Elinor...but no. She must have been through hell, finding herself unmarried and with child when he was sent away. He punched his leg in frustration. If he had only known. She must have thought herself unwanted. He cursed his youthful stupidity yet again.

Nathaniel met his cousin Andrew at Headquarters the next day, before he returned to Lydia.

"You have a daughter?" Andrew gaped open-mouthed, not bothering to hide his shock.

"Aye. Her name is Amelia."

"Good God. Lydia has hidden her all of these years? I cannot credit her with it. You are certain the child is yours?" Andrew asked wide-eyed.

"There can be no doubt whatsoever."

"Why does she tell you now?"

"She tried to tell me in London. Apparently, on reaching her majority last month, she decided to escape to France."

"Escape?"

He nodded. "Her uncle's affections," he said with revulsion. "However, she has only applied to me for monetary support for her and the child."

"Astonishing. What do you mean to do?"

"Marry her, of course."

"And return to England with a wife and a—how many years old?—

daughter? Oh, to see my uncle's face! Or better yet, my aunt's!" Andrew could not contain his amusement.

Nathaniel remained silent.

"When shall the happy event take place?"

"I mean to apply to the Duke to make it happen before our confrontation with Boney. I fear we have little time."

Andrew nodded his understanding, and took him in to see the Duke of Wellington.

This done, the Duke, never prolific with words, only said, "Yes. Best to do it now."

By the next day, Nathaniel had convinced the army chaplain to marry them. The wedding was to be held at the Protestant church and was attended by none other than the Duke of Wellington himself. Nathaniel thought it prudent to have the Duke's approval for validity, should something happen to him. His cousin Andrew attended as well as Nurse, Amelia, and Ajax.

Lydia could not believe what was happening. She had dreamt of this day for an age. However, the ceremony was not what she had envisioned many, many years ago—her in a plain dress, Nathaniel in a plain uniform, in an unknown church. She was still not sure this was the right thing to do, but she had endured much for Amelia's sake and hopefully this would be happier than living with her uncle's demands. Her daughter would now have a name and a father. She wanted to believe it was right.

Amelia found her way into Wellington's lap before the ceremony was over, using all of her charms on his Grace. Nathaniel and Lydia turned to see her in the Duke's arms and could not help but chuckle. The Duke was known for his susceptibility to a pretty face. The Duke winked and waved his hand for the ceremony to continue.

Lydia heard herself say *I will,* and found herself receiving a chaste kiss from Nathaniel. This news was received with exquisite happiness by their daughter, who proceeded to clap her hands and jump up and down, to Nurse's horror. Everyone else only laughed, and Nathaniel took Amelia in his arms and swung her around to her delight.

The Duke proffered his felicitations and his happiness at seeing the situation made to rights.

"I will let Uxbridge and Somerset know not to expect you till the morning." He winked at Nathaniel and took his leave with Andrew. Lydia had to look down to hide her embarrassment.

The new family made their way back to the small house, Amelia in her papa's arms. She had not thought beyond this moment. Lydia was uncertain of Nathaniel's expectations of the marriage bed, but she had loved him and was not sure that she did not love him still. It had to be more pleasant than anything her uncle had done, she reflected. Nathaniel might have to return to his regiment before he could think of such things anyway. She did her best to dispense with the awkwardness by suggesting they dine.

"Shall you stay for supper?"

"That sounds nice."

"We do not have a cook, so you will have to excuse me while I prepare something."

Nathaniel raised his eyebrows.

"You need not look so surprised. I have learned a thing or two out of necessity."

"I will help you. I, too, have learned a few things out of necessity, in the field." He looked around. "What is there to work with? I am afraid my skills are limited to eggs, meat and toast."

"Then your abilities surpass mine." She held up her hands with a smile. "I have learned to boil water for tea and throw meat and vegetables in a pot for stew." She found an apron and tied it over her dress.

Nathaniel shed his jacket, rolled up his sleeves and went to the pantry and the larder and brought out some armfuls of provisions. Lydia was embarrassed at the small supply of food, but they lived from day to day, unsure of what the future held. If Nathaniel noticed, he did not comment.

"It looks like we will have breakfast for supper." Nathaniel pronounced.

"Splendid. What can I do to help?"

As Nathaniel sliced pieces of bacon and placed them in a pan on the fire, he directed Lydia to crack some eggs and beat them in a bowl. She had not the slightest idea how to accomplish this task. She cracked her first egg, and the whites poured out everywhere.

"Oh, drat!" she exclaimed in frustration.

Nathaniel laughed and came over to show her. He placed his arms around her and held her hands as he demonstrated.

She found herself transported back to their easy relationship of more than six years prior. She unknowingly leaned back into his arms, and felt him lean into her as well. She inhaled a deep breath of his manly, woody smell. For now she was content to feel his safe arms around her. They stood in the comfortable embrace for several minutes, until they were interrupted by smoking bacon. Nathaniel only laughed and went to retrieve what he could of their supper. They were soon joined by Amelia and Nurse, and spent a pleasant evening playing spillikins and putting their daughter to bed.

Once alone, Lydia found herself feeling unaccountably shy. The only time she had been with Nathaniel she had not known what she was about. When her uncle had taken his liberties with her, she had numbed herself to all feeling and had tried to escape reality by thinking of her daughter. Now she knew what was expected but was unsure how to go about the act in the proper manner.

Nathaniel seemed to sense her hesitation. "I can remove to a hotel for the night. I dare not show my face back at camp before morning, though. I would never live it down." He laughed.

"You would never find a room this late. Besides, I do not wish for you to leave." It occurred to her that he might be as nervous as she was.

"Are you certain?" He stepped forward and looked her straight in the eye, searching, it seemed, for her true feelings. "I know this was rather sudden and I would never force anything on you that you were uncomfortable with."

"I know. Only I never thought to be with you again. I thought all was over…"

"Shh, I know." He took her face in his hands and kissed her tenderly, sending a rush of warmth through her. He stopped with that and only held her in his arms. Affection without expectations was foreign to Lydia. Did he not want her? She would save the doubts for the morrow and enjoy being held in his arms for now.

The night passed too quickly, and Nathaniel rose and dressed himself at daylight.

"Must you leave so soon?"

"Unfortunately, I must register our marriage at the embassy and see a solicitor before returning to my regiment. Napoleon cannot be far away now. The Duchess of Richmond is holding a ball three days from now. I would be pleased if you would join me there."

"Pardon? A ball? I have brought nothing fit for Society." Not to mention she feared her acceptance as his wife.

Nathaniel pulled a great number of bills from his pocket and placed them in her hand. "I realize it might be difficult to find something at short notice, but please do try." He flashed her a brilliant smile. "I wish to present my beautiful wife."

"Scoundrel."

Nathaniel's first order of business after registering the marriage at the embassy was to make his way to Headquarters. There, he wrote a letter to his father confessing the whole. He had no idea how the news would be received, but he would not keep this from him. News was bound to reach his ears soon, and he would prefer the true story to come from him. He then posted a letter to his solicitor, with a new Will, witnessed by his cousin Andrew and the Duke. He made a second copy and gave it to Andrew for safe-keeping.

"Please see that they are taken care of, if anything should happen."

"Come now. A cat would be jealous of your lives, Nate!" was Andrew's reply.

"Having something to live for changes my luck." Nathaniel was sombre.

"Nonsense."

"Promise me." Nathaniel thrust his face close to his cousin's, demanding his oath.

"Of course. I will do anything should it become necessary. But give Achilles a breather."

"I will do what I must. I do not know any other way."

"I know. Come through this alive."

"It is ironic. We face our fiercest battle yet, and now I suddenly have a reason to live."

Andrew had no reply. Nathaniel did not expect one. He tipped his cousin a quick salute and left Headquarters with a deep sense of foreboding. Everything in his life had changed in a few short days. He had never thought about living through a battle before, fighting without fear of death, and now his life had purpose, he was sure this would be his last. He felt better after the Will and letter to his father were taken care of, but that would still not make things easy for Lydia for a time.

It had been difficult to hold himself back with her, but he did not wish to take the chance of planting another child in her belly until he knew the outcome of this battle. His father would have argued with him on that point, but Lydia had suffered enough. Knowing he might have to leave a child behind without knowing him was already difficult to bear.

CHAPTER 10

$\mathcal{C}$ummins showed two Bow Street Runners into Lord Dannon's study, both of whom looked acutely uncomfortable in his lordship's presence.

"Well? I do not have all day! What have you found?" Lord Dannon demanded.

"We found her, and then lost her." The older Runner spoke, while the younger one fidgeted nervously.

"What do you mean you lost her?" He turned and marched over to the older Runner, and stood glaring at him.

"It seems she left London for Wiltshire after selling all of her jewels, my lord," the Runner replied with a nervous gulp.

"My country seat is in Wiltshire. Is she at my country house? That makes little sense, but who can guess a female's thoughts?" He walked over toward the window, pondering this revelation. He turned again sharply.

"Is she still there? Speak, man! What else have you?" he raged, his face red and veins bulging.

"We believe she has left the country, my lord."

"Left the country? This is madness! Are you certain?" He went over to pour another drink.

The Runner looked down at his notes and pretended to read, avoiding Lord Dannon's face. "She is believed to have boarded a ship bound for Dieppe, France, with another woman and a child." He shut the notebook.

Lord Dannon paced around the room again. He stopped in his tracks. "Son of a...." He turned back toward the Runner. "Did you say a child?"

"Yes, my lord."

"And who was this child?" he demanded.

"Beggin' your lordship's pardon, we did not have time to track down names. We came straight here to inform your lordship."

"Very well, I am informed. Now find them!"

"Yes, my lord. Us Runners won't let you down. We can unearth anything." They bowed and hurried out of the room.

"Then go do it!" he shouted after them. "She is weeks ahead of you by now!" He cursed under his breath, and hurled his drink into the hearth. The little whore had managed to find her daughter after all these years.

Lydia lay back down on the bed after Nathaniel had departed. She had not had time to reflect on the whirlwind of changes that had happened in a few days. Six years ago this marriage would have been a dream come true. She knew the marriage made their daughter legitimate, but that did not mean it would be easy for any of them to have her recognized in Society.

She had not truly believed Nathaniel would want anything to do with either of them, especially after his reaction to her at the ball. She was still shocked that he accepted Amelia and with such grace. He appeared to be genuinely pleased and enchanted by her. He had even insisted on kissing her goodbye that morning. She snuggled closer into the coverlet and thought about last night. Nathaniel holding her without any expectations meant more to her than she could find words to describe. Perhaps she should have been offended that he had not wanted to consummate the marriage, but no one had ever just held her before. He had even said their daughter was conceived in love. Could he really feel that way too? That, more than anything, gave her a glimmer of hope.

Nurse knocked on the door and brought in a tray with coffee and a roll. She glanced at her, trying to decide how she felt.

"You are looking rather pleased. I have not seen the bloom in your face in years."

"So has he been reduced from a limb of Satan?" Lydia asked, amused.

"I have yet to make up my mind. But he is headed the proper direction. I just pray this will not lead to more broken hearts." She shook her head.

"Mama, Mama! Where did Papa go?" Amelia burst into the room and hopped on the bed next to Lydia.

"He had to return to his regiment, love. He will be back to visit as soon as he can, I promise," Lydia said, receiving a warm hug from her daughter.

The little girl did her best not to be disappointed but her lower lip protruded anyway.

"Would you like to help Mama with some shopping today? Papa is going to take me to a fancy ball in three days, so I must find a dress."

"Three days?" Nurse exclaimed. "Impossible!"

"Difficult, not impossible," Lydia said to reassure herself as much as Nurse.

"You had best get up and about then, we have a busy day ahead of us."

They headed out towards the market on foot, Amelia in tow. She could never have shopped openly with a child in London, and she loved having Amelia with her. She was taking a risk, she knew, but at least she was married now.

Nurse continued to argue. "We will never have time to make a new dress," she exclaimed.

"Together we can manage." Lydia had become somewhat of an

expert seamstress, having had to re-sew gowns in order to save money.

They passed by a *modiste's* shop on their way to the silk warehouse. Lydia stopped. Did she dare try? There was a chance they would be seen this close to the ball. Lydia boldly turned.

"Whewe awe you going, Mama?"

"I, my love, am going to see if the *modiste* has anything ready-made. Your papa gave me money for a dress, and I am going to see if money truly talks."

"How can money talk?" The little girl wrinkled her face.

"It is a figure of speech, dear. If you have money, people will do things for you faster than they would do otherwise."

The little girl was still trying to understand this revelation when they entered the shop.

One of the shop assistants came over to help them but appeared unable to determine the lady's worth. Lydia could see the indecision on her face. Lydia had a nurse and child so she must think her of some rank, but the dress she wore was unremarkable. Nurse took Amelia to some chairs and sat quietly out of sight with her.

"May I help you?" she said in exquisitely proper French.

"*Oui, mademoiselle,*" Lydia answered. "I am in need of a dress for a ball in three days. I was unable to travel with my gowns, and I thought I would enquire if you had any dresses available. I realize it is difficult to make a dress at such short notice."

The girl seemed relieved that this lady was not asking the impossible. "I will check with *Madame.* One moment, please."

Several minutes later, the proprietress emerged from the back of the shop. She looked Lydia over, deep in thought. "Perhaps I have something that would suit. A lady ordered several gowns and left town without retrieving them."

Lydia looked toward the heavens with a quick prayer. She knew if the Duchess of Richmond was holding a ball that there had to be many others of Society who would be in attendance. She did not want to shame Nathaniel on their first appearance as a married couple.

The *Madame* returned with several gowns, and Lydia's eyes grew wide.

She first held up the most beautiful dress Lydia had ever seen. It was a midnight-blue gown with an extremely high, narrow waist. The skirt belled out slightly and was trimmed with three rows of white roses to match ones placed on the sleeves and trim of the bodice.

"You are married, no?" The *Madame's* eyes glanced subtly toward Amelia. The dark dress would not have been considered proper for an unmarried miss. Lydia had long ago dispensed with that convention. She refused to symbolize purity by wearing white. Her uncle had robbed her of any notions of purity she'd ever held.

"*Oui.*"

"Then this dress should do nicely. You are not so different in size from the one it was fashioned for. Should you like to try it?"

Lydia would have liked to have bounced up and down and clapped her hands, but chose to be proper. "Yes, of course."

When Lydia emerged from the dressing room wearing the gown, Nurse was no longer able to control Amelia.

"Oh, Mama! You look like a faiwy pwincess!"

Lydia remembered where they were and tried to shush Amelia. Fortunately the *Madame* was enchanted with the little girl. Lydia could not help but be amused. Her daughter seemed to have that effect on everyone she met.

The other gowns the *Madame* had brought out were displayed for Lydia. "Would you be interested in any of these which were also left?"

Lydia eyed the beautiful array of dresses displayed before her. She had enough money, but she had not been so indulgent in years. Did she dare? She was Lady Fairmont now. She would be expected to look the part, and she had brought only her plain, serviceable gowns with her. She had sold everything beautiful she had to finance their way here.

She nodded. The assistant attended Lydia and pinned the necessary alterations. Meanwhile, *Madame* had taken Amelia away and was measuring her for some new clothes. She knew when she had found gold.

Everyone prepared to leave, pleased with their success, and they made their way to purchase matching slippers, gloves and hats. As they exited the shop, they ran into Lady Georgiana Lennox, the Duchess of Richmond's daughter. Lydia nearly tripped when she saw her. She glanced toward Amelia, hoping that Nurse would take her in the other direction. Nurse did so, but not before Lady Georgiana caught sight of the child. She said nothing, but Lydia could see there was some recognition. Her manners were too proper to enquire, however.

"Lady Lydia," she said politely, "I did not know you were in Brussels."

"Lady Georgiana." They kissed each other on the cheek. They were not bosom friends, but they were acquainted. Lady Georgiana had always been kind to her.

"I have only just arrived."

"Do you stay long?"

"I suppose that depends on the war. I had intended to go to France but those plans were curtailed."

Lady Georgiana nodded understanding. "Are you with your aunt and uncle?"

Lydia knew Georgiana was asking because of the ball. She would have invited her if she had proper relatives to attend with her.

"No, I am with my other family." She chose not to specify. Lady Georgiana would find out soon enough.

Relief crossed Lady Georgiana's face. That must satisfy her curiosity about the child, Lydia thought.

They exchanged a few more pleasantries and said goodbye. Lydia hoped she had excused Amelia's presence, but there was nothing she could do about it now.

When the ladies returned from shopping, they were astonished to find three servants had been hired to help: a cook, a housekeeper, and a maid. Lydia was speechless.

"Bless his soul!" Nurse exclaimed. Nathaniel was no longer a limb of Satan, but an angel of the highest order.

"That did not take long," Lydia remarked.

"That wonderful husband of yours did not miss a thing!"

Lydia had to admit that, after a long month of deprivation, a little pampering was very welcome.

It was a good day indeed. Lydia had not been so happy or carefree in years. They had even managed to find a dress for the ball.

Nathaniel was unable to visit again prior to the fête, but he arrived early, and with a surprise for Amelia.

Lydia had yet to see Nathaniel in his full dress regimentals. He took her breath away. He did not seem displeased with her appearance either.

He took her hand and kissed it, then twirled her around to get a better look at her. From the pleased look in his eyes she blushed like a débutante. Her dress was cut in the Parisian fashion, which became her hourglass figure to perfection. The midnight-blue hue enhanced the brilliance of her eyes and complemented his regimentals. Nurse came in to the room and stopped short on the threshold. She had to dab away tears. Amelia rushed straight past Nurse and into his arms, crying, "Papa! Papa! You look like a pwince and pwincess. Oh, I wish I could go to the ball with you."

"Impossible, my love. But I did bring you a surprise."

"Where is it?" She squirmed out of his arms and began to search.

"I am afraid it is not in here. Come, I will show you."

He took her tiny hand in his and led her to the back alleyway, toward a nearby stable. There stood a beautiful pony and a dappled grey mare.

"A pony! A pony! Is it all mine?"

"I am afraid so." He knelt down to her level. "A pony is a very big responsibility. Are you certain you will be able to take care of him?"

Amelia nodded her head up and down. "Can I wide him now? Please, oh, please?"

There was no way to say no to those big grey eyes. "Only a quick ride. I must take your mama to the ball. The groom here will help you look after your pony and your mama's horse. He can lead you around a bit when I am not here, and when I come back, I will teach you. Does that sound acceptable to you?"

"Oh, yes, Papa!" He was rewarded with a big hug and a wet kiss on his cheek.

He looked toward Lydia. "Is Mama pleased with her horse too?"

"Oh, yes, Papa!" She stood on her tiptoes and planted a kiss on his other cheek.

Nathaniel led Amelia around on the pony for a few turns about the courtyard.

"That has to be all for now. It is time for your mama and me to go. I am not sure when I will be able to return. Will you look after your mama for me?"

Amelia looked up at her father and nodded. "I will, Papa."

"I knew you would." He gave her a kiss and held on to her tightly. He inhaled the fresh scent of her, memorizing it to get him through this war. He reluctantly handed his daughter to Nurse and held out his arm for Lydia to accompany him. He had so much to make up for.

Lydia was sad to see the disappointment on Amelia's face as they drove off, but she felt like Cinderella herself as her handsome prince drove her to the ball. She could not quite fathom her new life. She had dreamt of just this moment for years, but the reality was bitter-sweet. Knowing Nathaniel had only married her for their daughter was honourable, and she was glad for Amelia, but a part of her wished he had wanted to marry her for *her*. Lydia realized she had been wool-gathering and snapped herself back to the present. She looked over to Nathaniel sitting beside her in the carriage and he had an amused look on his face.

"Care to tell me what you were thinking?"

"It was nothing. I am still a bit astonished at how things have turned out after six years."

"I am sorry you were left to deal with everything on your own,

Lydia. I hope when this war is finished that I might make some of it up to you."

She shook her head. "There is nothing to make up for. All that matters now is Amelia."

"I disagree." He took her hand and got down on one knee in the carriage.

"What are you doing?"

"I know I made a mull of my proposal the other day, but I hope you will remember the first time I proposed." He chuckled. "No, I did not do it properly then, either." He pulled a ring from his pocket. "There were not many choices here at the moment."

Nathaniel placed a beautiful oval-shaped sapphire on her hand. The simplicity of the ring compared to the gaudy baubles her uncle had given her was a welcome contrast. Nathaniel had required no services for his affections on their wedding night. A hopeful fore-telling for their future, she hoped.

"I do not know what to say. Thank you."

"I did not wish for the marriage to look unwanted or in haste. I hope everyone will believe we have been betrothed all these years."

"I am doubtful of such ease of acceptance. Perhaps your reputation will carry us far. My reputation, however, is not so worthy. I confess, I was desperate when you left and I found myself increasing. Had your note led me to expect a continuation of your affection or hope for the future, I might have written to you. I knew I had no choice other than to try to find another husband. I had no expectation of your returning to wed me." She had to stop to compose herself.

"I wish things had been different, Lydia."

She nodded and looked away, as tears welled up in her eyes.

"I left because of what I had done to Elinor. I had no notion that you were increasing. I hoped my note would allow you to forget me. I cannot change the past, however, and can only hope to make the future better. For tonight, I trust you will allow me to dote on the new Lady Fairmont. If everyone believes we are in love, there will be fewer questions."

"I think I can manage to do so." There would be no pretending. She was not ready to give her heart completely to him, for all he held such a large piece of it already.

The carriage slowed as they took their place in line along the Rue de la Blanchesserie, awaiting their turn to alight. They walked toward the old carriage house on the warm, sultry June night. Nathaniel handed a card to the butler, then reached over and gave Lydia a kiss on the cheek. "Smile. It is our turn."

The butler announced, "My Lord and Lady Fairmont."

CHAPTER 11

15 JUNE 1815

*N*athaniel expected a few hushed whispers and raised eyebrows, but he did not expect the entire ballroom to turn and stare silently. You could have heard a pin drop. Many turned to their neighbour, as if to see if they had heard the names properly. Not only did it appear their marriage had come as a surprise, but the couple made a stunning picture standing atop the entrance, as witnessed by their reflection in an ornate pier-glass. Nathaniel often turned heads, but even more so in his red dress regimentals. Lydia, too, was breathtaking in her deep-blue hue that outshone the more demure of the female ensembles. Nathaniel broke the silence by walking on toward the hosts.

"You remember my lovely wife, Lady Fairmont? I do hope you will forgive my assumption that my wife would be welcome." Nathaniel smiled with devastating effect as he greeted his host and hostess.

The Duchess of Richmond could barely recover herself to respond to his pronouncement. "Of course, Lady Fairmont, you are most welcome." When the Duchess of Richmond found her wits, she welcomed them as if nothing were abnormal in Lord Fairmont's arrival with a bride.

"Thank you, your Grace," Lydia replied in a voice that was appropriately demure.

He hoped people assumed the couple had married in England when he was home and had brought his new bride along to follow the drum. The older matrons recalled they had been together several years ago. The crowd began to mingle and dance again, chattering in speculation about the Fairmonts. The gossip was short-lived however, with the news of war on their doorstep circulating.

The couple proceeded into the old carriage house-turned-ballroom that had been dressed with wallpaper, fragrant floral ornamentation and glowing candelabras. The hot night was not conducive to a stuffy room and formal dress. Thankfully, the windows had been opened, but provided little relief to the wilting shirt points and cravats. They were greeted by some of Nathaniel's regiment who were unacquainted with Lydia, and were pleased to offer her their congratulations and solicit the beauty's hand for a dance. Their leader was disobliging, however, and kept his new bride to himself.

Lydia might not realize the danger they were in, but he was all too aware. Nathaniel had received orders shortly before leaving to go to her. They were to march immediately after the festivities ceased; the ball was to proceed in order to subdue the panic that would shortly ensue. When they had arrived, many of the royalty of the Allied Army was present, but Wellington himself had not yet made an appearance, which left a tenor of uneasiness that was thinly masked by the merriment of a dance.

Nathaniel looked out over the crowd. Scottish bagpipes began to play, and the crowd parted to the Royal Highlanders dancing to one of their own tunes for the crowd's pleasure. He grinned; quite a spectacle they made in their kilts and sporrans with their swords swinging! They were treated to several dances—reels, sword dances, and strathspeys—to the delight of everyone present, a momentary diversion from the underlying emotions of the evening.

As the Highlanders retired from the dance floor, the orchestra struck up a waltz. Nathaniel led out his blooming bride. Young officers began dancing with every willing miss in sight with the need to expend their nervous rush of excitement at finally getting to see action; the more seasoned chose to gather and speculate, the gravity of the forthcoming event not lost on them.

Nathaniel recalled the youthful exuberance he had once felt before any clash; many of those dancing gaily there tonight would not live to see another day. The irony of the two extremes of war and pleasure was brought home to him, and he would savour every moment he had Lydia in his arms. If nothing else, he hoped to leave her with a good memory of their last night together.

He found he was nervous as he put his hand on her waist. He had danced a few times as this was one of the requirements of Wellington's officers, of course, but never had feelings entered into any of them before. He had never allowed that. He realized he would have to change his outlook when this war was over. Perhaps this was God's new challenge to him.

"You look beautiful, Lydia." He was struggling to find words, but he wanted her to know how he felt.

"Thank you." She looked down at the trim on his tunic, obviously trying not to blush.

"No matter what happens, I want you to hold your head high for Amelia's sake."

"You are talking awfully morbidly, Nathaniel."

"One never knows when you will have tomorrow, especially in my present occupation. I have seen more death than you can fathom."

"I wish you would not speak so. I have only just found you again."

"I must speak thus, though I am loath to do so. You may not realize the enormity of the conflict before us, but I have been fighting Napoleon almost six years. I am certain this is the grand finale, and I cannot guarantee the outcome."

Lydia faltered in the dance. Nathaniel continued, "I have written to my father and my solicitor to inform them of our marriage. You shall not want for anything again, Lydia. If I have done nothing else to make things right, I am hopeful that some of your hardships may be alleviated, at least."

She refused to look him in the face as tears filled her eyes.

"I will not request you return to England, if that is not your wish. But, if the outcome of the battle is not favourable for England and I do not return, my uncle has land in Virginia that you would be welcomed to."

"In America?"

He nodded. She remained silent. He realized this upcoming battle would be no ordinary one. He looked out across the ballroom and unconsciously pulled Lydia closer. It was as if they were moving as one in slow motion. There were an inordinate number of waltzes played that night, but no one paid any heed, the whole evening seeming to be an exception to the rule.

As they danced, it felt like heaven to be in Nathaniel's arms again. Lydia glided as lightly on her feet as she had when she had been a naïve débutante. She was swept away in a euphoric haze, ignorant of what was going on around her, until Nathaniel took the wind out of her sails with his talk of being killed.

They danced time after time, both more quiet and reserved after the earlier conversation. She refused to think of the consequences now and tried to enjoy the present.

"Who is Andrew dancing with?"

Lydia returned her attention to her husband. "Where is he?"

Nathaniel nodded toward his right. "Circling in front of the alcove."

"I did not know they were in Brussels! That is one of the Ashbury triplets."

She could see him searching for recognition.

"I believe they were raised in France. They came out in London this past Season."

"The name is familiar, but I was a bit preoccupied whilst in England."

"I had noticed."

The dance finished. It was sweltering in the ballroom, and they walked toward the refreshments, then made their way toward the terrace. Apparently they were not the only ones with the same idea.

Lady Georgiana was outside, speaking to Lord Hay. She appeared to be quite irritated with him. "How could you?" they overheard her say.

She noticed her audience and greeted the Fairmonts. "Congratulations, Lord and Lady Fairmont. Everything suddenly makes more sense," she said as she looked to Lydia with a smile.

"Forgive me for the secrecy, Georgy."

Lady Georgiana waved her hand. "Nonsense. There is nothing to forgive. I would have done the same." She smiled kindly and went back to chastising Lord Hay.

They made their way over to where Andrew was speaking to one of the Ashbury girls.

Andrew greeted his cousin and Lydia warmly, and made introductions.

"Colonel Lord Fairmont, may I present Lady Margaux Winslow."

"Congratulations, my lord; my lady."

"Thank you. What brings you to Brussels?"

"My brother is also in the army, and we needed to take a holiday from England." She looked shyly toward Andrew and flushed. Lydia could only guess what the flush was for; Lady Margaux was being openly courted by Lord Vernon when she herself had left England. She drew Andrew over to her to converse with him, while Nathaniel spoke to Lady Margaux about her brother. Lydia wondered how her friend Lady Beatrice was doing in Scotland.

"Have you any word on Beatrice? I have forgotten to ask Nathaniel."

"I came directly from Scotland. She was staying at Vernon's hunting box."

"No! That sounds dreadfully awkward. I would have hoped he chose to ignore his obsession with pheasants this year."

"Unfortunately not. He arrived with the entire Ashbury clan in tow."

Lydia felt sorry for Beatrice. That was the worst sort of humiliation she could imagine.

"They decided they would not suit, however. I imagine Lady Beatrice's presence was too much for Lady Margaux. Vernon could not subconsciously hide his feelings. I left there hopeful for reconciliation. And you will be pleasantly surprised by the change in Bea."

"Poor Lady Margaux, then. What a mess!"

"I am as surprised as you to see them here."

"Pleasantly surprised, I would think." She gave him a knowing smile. "You never seem to lack for a dancing partner when they are present."

"Yes, I am happy to dance with all of them."

She gave him a confused look. "They seem to adore you equally."

"Yes, much like they adore their beloved brother."

She nudged him slightly in the arm. "Doubtful, Major Abbott, doubtful."

It was some time after midnight when Wellington arrived. The great man himself came over to publicly congratulate the pair and give his blessing.

"Good evening, sir." Nathaniel greeted his commander.

"Ah, the newly wed Fairmonts. Good evening. My felicitations."

"Thank you, your Grace." Lydia smiled and curtsied.

The Duke winked at her and was drawn away by people wanting to know if the rumours about the French were true. He attempted to portray an outward sense of calm, but those who knew him best knew that it was an act for the public benefit. He was approached by, and likewise summoned, his leading officers as they passed him. Each time he announced that he had 'no plans!' or no news of import, other than they must be in place in the morning.

Not long after the Duke's arrival, many of the soldiers began to take their leave to join their regiments before the party sat down to supper.

The Prince of Orange, who had left earlier with the Duke of Brunswick, returned and frantically sought out the Duke with a dispatch. The entire room kept their eyes on this interchange, waiting for news. It was not the Duke's style, however, to announce his plans publicly, and he merely said he had no fresh orders for His Royal Highness.

The message could only mean one thing, Nathaniel knew: Napoleon had arrived.

The effect on the crowd was sobering. The Duke finished his present conversation, and then took leave of his hostess. Lord Uxbridge pulled Nathaniel aside to relay orders.

"Your regiment is gathering at Nivelles as ordered?

Nathaniel nodded, "Yes. Has the order changed?"

"We are to concentrate on Quatre-Bras. I will set up headquarters in Waterloo. We will rendezvous there later this morning. See your bride home safely, first." He raised an intrigued eyebrow at Nathaniel, but would receive no more enlightenment on his curious marriage. Nathaniel could see Lydia watching this interchange with growing trepidation. He returned to her side shortly.

"I have been called away. I will escort you home, and then I must be off."

"So soon?"

"Immediately."

Nathaniel had little speech available to him other than the trivial niceties when taking leave of their hostess. Lydia was equally quiet. The ride home was short. He pulled her close and held her, letting his feelings show through action, his emotions too raw for words.

He walked Lydia into the house. He crept quietly into Amelia's bedroom and lingered a few minutes looking at his angelic daughter, memorizing her every feature. He bent over to kiss Amelia one more time and then hurried from her room.

"When will we see you again?" she asked when they had walked to the door.

"I do not know." He saw the fear and disappointment on her face. "I wish I knew."

She nodded through her tears, trying to maintain strength so he would not worry about them. He wiped the tears from her cheek.

He kissed Lydia goodbye more roughly than he intended, allowing his feelings to get the better of him. He pulled her into his arms, "Goodbye, my love." Then he turned to leave before he lost all control.

~

Lydia watched Nathaniel go. Was her fairy tale over with as quickly as it had begun? She did not want to consider losing Nathaniel, just as surely as she had found him again. Could Fate be so cruel? She had to stop these thoughts. She would not borrow worries. He was a seasoned veteran, she knew. Perhaps all soldiers felt this way before battle. He had never had a family to worry about, and now he had a wife and child within the span of one week.

Lydia was tired, but could no more entertain thoughts of sleeping than Nathaniel could. She knew not what any of this meant. She had no notion of war other than her education in the daily newspapers, and no source for information—though they were literally on war's doorstep.

She heard horns blow, followed by a loud, repetitive thumping noise. She was startled, but opened the door and began mindlessly walking toward the noise to see what it was about. She only had to walk along a few streets towards the Place Royale to find the square bustling with activity, despite the dawn just beginning to break. There were soldiers everywhere—some she had even that night seen dancing at the ball—forming up in their squadrons and regiments to the call of the drums.

She stood there watching, lost to all sense of time and place. The war really was on their doorstep, not something that was only the myth and legend of books. She had never felt so lost—or alone. Were they safe to stay in Brussels? Nathaniel had not warned her to leave. Surely he would have done so if it were not safe. She would have to find some source of news tomorrow. For now, she turned and walked back to her small home and held her daughter tight as she slept, hoping she had done the right thing. The heart that had just given itself completely to Nathaniel was perilously close to breaking.

CHAPTER 12

16 JUNE 1815

*I*t was oddly quiet, save the beating of the drums calling the soldiers to action, as Nathaniel left Lydia and his daughter behind in the small house on the Rue de Madeleine. The dawn was creeping over the square as he led his horse from the stable. He stood there for a moment and watched the young men, many of them not yet old enough to shave, march with their muskets and knapsacks toward the southern gate of the city. The Highlanders who had been at the ball were chanting their battle cry and playing their fifes as they marched. The citizens stood quietly watching this spectacle, probably afraid of what losing this war would mean for them and their city. Many had billeted soldiers and were watching their friends say farewell for the last time.

Never before had Nathaniel wanted to walk away from a battle, from his calling. A true warrior, he lived for these moments. But every part of his being was screaming at him to stay by his wife and daughter's sides. He fought his inner turmoil, however; he would do his duty. Fear of death had no place in a soldier's thoughts during battle. Allowing Bonaparte to win, to take over, was a worse option than losing Nathaniel. Oh, the irony. Death would have been welcomed these six years past, and now he wanted to live. The fact that Bonaparte had a stolen twenty-four-hour march on Wellington was not a good omen for the outcome of the fight.

Once through the Namur gate, he mounted his horse and rode to join his regiment with overwhelming melancholy. The feeling of riding into battle was difficult to put into words, but his normal rush of anticipation was not present. He spent most of the way conversing with himself, trying to assemble some sense out of the occurrences of the last week and reflecting if his choices had been correct. He felt a measure of peace knowing that Lydia and Amelia would be provided for, and even a small measure of relief knowing that Elinor had forgiven him.

He spurred his horse forward, despite his misgivings, as the sun began to rise over the tall birches and lush fields of rye and barley. The countryside suddenly grew eerily quiet, the calm before the storm.

It did not last long. Before he made it to Uxbridge's headquarters in the village of Waterloo, he heard fire fight break out in the south. There would be no time to dwell on anything other than survival. He hoped enough of the Army had been assembled to hold Boney off until the masses were in place. He arrived at the designated rally point on the morning of the sixteenth. Lord Somerset and Lord Uxbridge were only now arriving themselves. None had had the luxury of changing out of their dress uniforms yet. Nathaniel pulled up his horse and reported to receive orders.

"Sir." Nathaniel saluted Lord Uxbridge and Lord Somerset upon arriving. "What is the fire-fight I hear?"

"The Prince of Orange, Picton, Alten and Brunswick are engaged with the French at Quatre Bras. Wellington has gone to take over. We will wait in reserve for orders."

The orders came in late, as there was some confusion, but the cavalry arrived in time to help defeat the French, but not without loss. General Picton was hurt and his regiment severely lessened; Lord Hay and the Duke of Brunswick were killed along with most of the High-landers. The cavalry remained to occupy the area as the re-enforcements continued to build and position themselves for the main conflict. The Anglo-Dutch army had managed to hold the French off for the moment.

"Wellington does not wish to fight Napoleon at Quatre-Bras. The positioning would put us at a strong disadvantage."

"So we retreat and wait?" Nathaniel asked. "I agree the spot is not ideal."

"He prefers the area near Mont St. Jean, about two miles to the south of Waterloo," Uxbridge answered.

"Draw Boney to us. That sounds like him."

"That is why he is the great man. That, and his possessing the luck of the devil!"

"Better him than me," Nathaniel replied.

Lydia was going to lose her mind. She could not sit in the parlour and wait until someone took pity and called on them. Did one still even make social calls during a war? She thought it doubtful, but would be queer in the attic if she did not hear something soon. She had to find a source for news. The suspense was more than she could bear, but whenever she went near the places ladies frequented in an effort to acquire information, she would leave frustrated. Those who had connections to the war knew little, and those who did not were oblivious to the plight of the ones left behind, being more concerned about frivolous gossip than the men fighting for their lives. Even in England she had been aware of Nathaniel out there fighting somewhere. Her respect grew for the wives who kept everything in order at home while their men were away. She did not know if she could bear that when this war ended.

She decided she would have to try asking in a café. She walked to the Grand Place where she had seen such establishments, where men gathered and sat for hours talking about politics and news. In England, she had never considered going into such an establishment, but times were desperate and the rules seemed different here. She entered cautiously and looked about for a friendly face.

The only person who took notice of her was an elderly gentleman with white hair and moustache. He had a kind smile.

"*Hallo, juffrow,*" The old man said with a tip of his hat.

Was he speaking Dutch? She knew no Dutch words. "*Parlez-vous francais?*"

"*Oui.* Are you looking for someone?"

"No, I am seeking news about the war."

"There is little news to be had." He shook his head.

She looked as disappointed as she felt. This waiting and not knowing was putting her on edge.

"Are you here alone?"

"Not alone, but there is no one to find information for me."

"They say there will be no action for days. The Allied forces need more time to accumulate their troops in one place."

Lydia did not know if this was welcome news or no. It would be longer until she could rest easy and see Nathaniel again. "*Merci, monsieur.* That is more than I knew."

"I am here every day at this time. I will tell you if I hear of anything. My son, he fights, too. I am also anxious to know."

She nodded and held out her hand to the kind stranger. "Lydia Fairmont."

"Aart Groendyke." He accepted her hand and shook heartily.

"Until tomorrow, *monsieur.*"

Lydia was sobered as she walked along the streets toward home. They were no longer filled with laughing people and playing children, but quiet, sombre faces preparing for the aftermath of war. The streets were lined with baggage wagons and carts in preparation for the wounded. Tents were being raised as infirmaries, while a call went out for bandages and flint to pack and dress wounds. Lydia cringed inwardly. How morbid this business was.

She returned home and told Amelia and Nurse the little news she had. Amelia was disappointed, but took it with the grace of a five-year-old. She moved on to her dolls, her kitten and then to her pony.

"Do you think we should move out of Brussels? Will it be safe for us to remain?" Nurse asked after Amelia was out of earshot.

"Nathaniel said nothing about moving, and I assume he would have warned us. Especially with having her here."

"I pray you are right, but he was rather occupied and everything happened very quickly."

"Too quickly," Lydia agreed quietly. She prayed she had done the right thing.

Nurse began to fidget—never a good sign. "Perhaps we should consider moving on to Antwerp until the danger passes."

"I will not leave unless ordered to do so."

"I was afraid you would say that."

The next day, the seventeenth of June, Uxbridge and the cavalry occupied the area around the village of Genappe and found French lancers scouting. The English Hussars had never before encountered lancers, and could do little to fend them off as they wielded terribly efficient ten-foot poles with steel points during a charge. The leader of the squadron that was formerly Nathaniel's was mortally wounded and taken prisoner.

Nathaniel received this news with pain, a reminder to keep his attention on the task at hand, as he waited in reserve for his turn to advance with the Life Guards. The order soon came from Uxbridge, and the Life Guards made a forceful approach favoured by a slope and were able to drive the lancers back into the village of Genappe. Lord Somerset followed, charging with the remainder of the Household Brigade, and they were engaged for some time, holding back the French. A wild thunderstorm broke out over the area during the pursuit, making conditions near impossible with the wet, muddy soil and beating rains. The remainder of engaged forces were ordered to retreat north and bivouac for the night. Uxbridge, with his cavalry brigades, made a stand, but was himself soon forced to retreat.

As Nathaniel rode alongside Lord Uxbridge and Lord Somerset, heading north through the storm, they reviewed the skirmish.

"That was only posturing for our benefit," Uxbridge remarked.

"Aye. And scouting, I'm sure," Somerset agreed.

"One positive is the Life Guards are now initiated and ready for the real battle," Uxbridge commented.

"Indeed. Let us hope they can perform so valiantly when the true test comes. A short battle is not the same as hours upon hours." Nathaniel was encouraged, but still not convinced.

"I have no worries. If they proved themselves in the mud, they can persevere. You are doing well with them," Uxbridge complimented Nathaniel's leadership.

"Thank you, sir. I cannot help but feel that the Rifles heckling them kept them going."

Uxbridge and Somerset laughed. "Once they learned not to run to the back of the line as soon as they were splattered with mud, they got on brilliantly." They continued to laugh, but their conversation was halted by pouring rains.

Once back at Headquarters, they attempted to dry off and find a meal.

Andrew was waiting there to brief Uxbridge with orders from the Duke.

"Let us change and sit at the table for our news, unless it cannot wait."

Andrew shook his head. "A meal would be welcome, sir."

Once seated near a fire with a meal and glass of brandy to warm them, Uxbridge requested the news.

"Wellington learned of the Prussian defeat at Ligny this morning. He immediately ordered a withdrawal to Mont St Jean. He said if he could be certain of the support of at least two Prussians corps he would do battle there."

"Just as we thought. Are the Prussians to join us then?"

"The main of them retreated to Wavre. Wellington has sent orders for them to fill in the right."

"I collect we are unsure if they will make it."

"Yes, sir." Andrew pulled out a written missive from the Duke and handed it to Uxbridge. He scanned the document and looked up.

"I must go to the Duke to review positioning. I suggest you all attempt to rest, for I expect tomorrow will be unlike any other. Do you stay here tonight, Fairmont?"

"Nay, I'm off to my troops."

Uxbridge wrinkled his nose. "I have never understood your desire to punish yourself, but I suppose that is why your men respect you as they do."

Uxbridge took his leave. Andrew rose to return to Wellington's headquarters, offering his opinion that he anticipated more dispatches would need to be delivered through the night.

"Are you headed toward Brussels?" Nathaniel asked.

"I am unsure. Do you want me to call on Lady Lydia?"

"It would relieve my mind. She is likely worried and has no one to ask."

"Shall I tell her to remove to Antwerp?"

He shook his head. "I doubt it would do any good."

Word of the retreat had sent panic through the hearts of the Bruxellois, and sent the city into chaos. A Belgian cavalry unit had raged through the city warning of the French's coming and impending victory. Andrew made his way slowly towards the city through rain and mud. The Brussels-Charleroi road had been clogged, crowded with overturned carts and broken wheels dislodged during the mad rush to safety. He made it much later than expected, drenched and cold, and sought the small house occupied by Lydia.

Thunder had echoed from a distance all that afternoon, and by dark a severe storm struck during the night. He was relieved to finally make it to the house. He only hoped someone would be awake to receive him. He knocked on the door, and Lydia herself appeared before him.

"Major Abbott! I was not expecting you. Please come in!"

"Thank you." Andrew stepped inside, happy to be out of the rain.

"You are drenched! Let us put your boots and coat by the fire. I regret I have no dry clothes to give you."

"I am quite used to these conditions. I do not intend to stay long."

"Let me at least find you a towel and drink to warm you."

Lydia went off to find these items before he could object and returned shortly. Andrew mopped himself with the towel and drank the warm tea laced with brandy greedily.

"Have you seen Nathaniel, by chance?"

"Forgive me. I should have eased your anxieties straight away. All was well when I left him. He sent me to call on you, you know."

Lydia sighed with relief. "Thank you for doing so. Surely you did not ride all this way only for me?"

Andrew looked away, feeling guilty. He had. He knew Nathaniel would not be easy unless he knew of their safety.

"Has the battle begun?"

"Aye. At Quatre-Bras yesterday. The Guards did famously, even though they were covered with mud."

"That is good news. I would have been more worried had I known."

"Unfortunately, we sustained some dear losses otherwise. The Duke of Brunswick and Lord Hay fell."

"Oh, dear." Lydia fought away tears.

Andrew thought of the two men whom she had danced near at the ball only two nights previously. It seemed a lifetime ago. He knew knowing the people who died made it more real.

"The cavalry was able to hold off French lancers at Genappe this afternoon, but the main battle is expected on the morrow."

Lydia sucked in her breath.

"We were obliged to retreat to Mont St Jean whilst trying to draw the French to us and awaiting the remainder of our forces. They are bivouacking there for the night."

"In this storm?" Lydia's face showed astonishment.

"Oh, it always rain for Wellington's battles. We have come to expect it. I must be off. The chaos of earlier has clogged the roads badly. I will return when I can."

"Thank you for coming, Major Abbott."

~

Lydia was certain she was not at all suited to being an army wife. The next day was quiet for a while, though anticipation hung like an ominous cloud. Lydia realized now the sounds she had thought were thunder had been a fierce gun battle followed by an actual storm. Brussels soon saw the wounded begin to flood through the gates. Everyone was pulled in to help. It seemed as though the hurt were everywhere—some had walked all the way from Waterloo in their wounded state. Doors were thrown open; Lydia could do naught but assist, ordering Nurse to keep Amelia inside away from the horrors on the streets.

She found herself stunned into action. She'd never had cause to have experience with injuries, but she found herself immediately needed. Sisters of mercy were out helping and gave her directions on how to assist. She only had to look about her to find someone in need —a drink of water here, a strip of her petticoat to bind a wound there, helping the injured to the shade or procuring a bit of brandy for pain over there. The only time she gave thanks to her uncle was for giving her the ability to numb herself to her surroundings for a time. She did not have time to think about being ill; her discomfort was a mere trifle to the needs of these wounded and dying men.

When she finally had time to stop and rest for a moment, she found that the day was quite advanced. She was light-headed and feverish from being out in the sweltering heat the entire day. The soldiers had been out there all day and all night, she reminded herself. *Nathaniel had been too.* She pressed onward, though the skies had opened and her gown was soaked through. She refused to give up, fearing she would find Nathaniel among the wounded without anyone to help him.

CHAPTER 13

18 JUNE 1815

The next morning, the bugles and drums began sounding around five o'clock. A heavy mist lay low over the valley, the remains of a rain-soaked night. It had finally stopped, but the aftermath of the deluge remained. The soldiers were damp and shivering, exhausted from a wet, sleepless night. There had been nowhere to escape the rain. Nathaniel had sat near the fire through most of the night, unable to sleep. His officers began to join him and they quietly partook of their rations of breakfast.

By nine, Wellington had been to inspect the position and make final alterations. His aides-de-camp rode furiously in every direction with his orders. The mist swirled away, and they began to see the blue uniforms of the French assemble across the ridge as they continued their own preparations.

By half past ten, all were in place for the epic battle. It was a formidable vision. Nathaniel looked out over the valley for at least a mile. Each army occupied opposing ridges: the French were spread out in a sea of blue from La Belle-Alliance, arranged in columns of Ws, and the majority of the Allied Army were hidden from view to the right of the farm, La Haye Sainte, only one brigade fully exposed. The Allied position had been carefully examined by the Duke during a reconnaissance the year before, and gave them that advantage. In the centre of the battlefield, running from south to north, was the Charleroi-Brussels road. The ground was a muddy mess, the day promising to be sweltering, and they waited for the French to make their move. And waited. There had been no sign of movement for half an hour. The Life Guards had been in position too long and began lounging about.

"What are they waiting for?" an impatient officer asked.

Nathaniel looked through his glass, over at the enemy. They stood ready and silent. No sooner had the words been spoken than the scream of the first cannon resounded through the valley.

Andrew rode by on his way to deliver a message to Lord Hill, but pulled up quickly when he spotted Nathaniel's regiment.

"Did you see her?" Nathaniel asked anxiously.

"I did. All was well. You were correct. She had no desire to leave Brussels without you."

"I am indebted to you, Andrew."

"Just see that you are able to take her from Brussels yourself. Godspeed."

Andrew tipped his hat and rode on.

Their brigade was readied in three columns behind the infantry of Ompteda and Keilmannsegge, just to the west of the farm of La Haye Sainte. The battle raged for over two hours before the Household Brigade was called upon. Patience was not Nathaniel's greatest virtue in battle; he preferred action. Lord Uxbridge had been given a free hand with his cavalry, and at last he gave the word. The Household Brigade and the Union Brigade attacked simultaneously. Nathaniel led his men slowly through the sunken road to their front. There was confusion in the colours of uniforms about who to attack, so the brigades became intermingled, and many made their own strategic decisions. They were ordered back to re-form.

Uxbridge then told the Union Brigade to charge, while he took the Household Brigade to relieve the pressure on the battle-scarred La Haye Sainte.

Unfortunately, in doing so, the Household Brigade had scattered itself. Uxbridge himself fell back in an attempt to gather help, but found few cavalrymen available. Many had advanced so far that they had a difficult time breaking back through the French lines to return to their own side. The fighting continued for some time, and packets of Household Brigade rode between the defiant British squares and even helped to rescue an endangered infantry unit.

Uxbridge witnessed the slaughter, and fearing that the French cavalry might overwhelm Keilmannsegge's Brigade, he sent Somerset's Household Brigade forward to drive off the French *Cuirassiers*. Nathaniel led the charge, flying fearlessly into the heart of the battle. His regiment drove the *Cuirassiers* back down the slope. The French then turned north down the road, trying to make their escape, Nathaniel and his Guards close on their heels and harassing them all the way.

Another band of French infantry, that had been taking refuge in the kitchen garden of the farm, attacked, and Nathaniel's unit destroyed it. On descending the forward slope, the Life Guards of his squadron met and charged though a line of French *Cuirassiers,* killing or wounding most of them, and then found themselves in the midst of a multitude of French infantry, most of whom threw themselves on the ground as soon as they realized they were under attack. They lay flat and hoped the horses would not tread upon them. These Frenchmen then shot the cavalrymen in the back after they had passed.

Hours passed in this way, Nathaniel led his regiment in charge after charge. Many of the British cavalry busied themselves chasing the less experienced French soldiers back and forth across the slope and dispensing with the easier victims. There were numerous knots of French soldiers who formed rallying squares to fend off the British cavalry. As the battle raged on, the losses to the Household Brigade were becoming heavy. Nathaniel watched soldier after soldier fall before him and forced himself to go on.

The air had become so thick with smoke from gunfire that it was difficult to see or breathe. A fierce fire raged to the west at the Château Hougoumont, making the conditions worse. He forced himself to stop for a drink and to rally his men. Andrew was racing by again and he called out to him.

"Abbott!"

Andrew pulled up and turned about cautiously, avoiding a fallen body. He pulled near to Nathaniel, who was seeking the shade of a tree in the orchard.

"How are things?" Nathaniel asked, hoping for news of relief on the way.

"Between you and me, I do not know. General Picton was killed. He was still wearing his civilian clothes."

Nathaniel cringed. Picton was not well liked, but he was a fine soldier.

"How are your Guards holding up?"

Nathaniel shook his head. "It is a nasty business out there."

Lord Uxbridge chose that moment to order his British cavalry to advance. Nathaniel jumped to and rallied his remaining troops. They charged down on the French once again, routed more *Cuirassiers*, then plunged into the mass of the French infantry while the Union Brigade charged on other columns. The French panicked and ran after a fierce struggle.

The Union Brigade, led by Ponsonby, continued and charged the French in the valley. Although they reached the guns and killed many artillerymen, their charge was doomed. Napoleon sent in a *Cuirassier* brigade and lancers to make a counter attack. Ponsonby was killed and his brigade was cut to pieces.

Wellington used the time won by his heavy cavalry to reinforce La Haye Sainte, reoccupy the sand-pit and bring up a reserve brigade into the line.

Late in the afternoon they faced another fierce charge by the French. They seemed determined to take the farm of La Haye Sainte, the heart of the Allied force. The more numerous French guns gained the upper hand and pounded the Allied centre. Wellington ordered his line to retreat behind the crest of the plateau. He summoned units from his right and left to rebuild his devastated middle.

Long columns of wounded soldiers started marching toward Brussels. Seeing these movements through the thick wall of smoke that hung over the battlefield, the French must have assumed they were retreating. The French sent their cavalry against the least damaged part of the Allied line.

"What is he doing sending his cavalry in without support? There is no infantry or artillery to back them up!" Somerset shouted.

"Do not question our luck, but thank God!" Uxbridge replied.

Nathaniel did not know how much longer their forces could last. They were decimated. They were hindered by the soft, wet ground, and the passage over the sunken roads littered with dead and wounded was becoming impassable. The cavalry was used up and most of his artillery was in bad shape.

What remained of the infantry was re-formed into squares. Without enough room and speed, the momentum of the French charges were broken. The horsemen swept around the squares, trying to penetrate them. Uxbridge's cavalry continued to make counter attacks and send the French back down the slope.

The sun was now far into the western sky, and the French had worked up close to the farm. Two Allied battalions sent to reinforce the farm were caught by French *Cuirassiers*. Uxbridge and the cavalry managed to save one, but it suffered heavy losses. The other battalion was destroyed. The French were able to capture La Haye Sainte in a fierce assault, and the survivors ran for their lives. The Allied infantry took another heavy beating. The remainder of the Allied cavalry tried to do what they could, but they were done. Cavalry regiments refused to charge again, and some even ran away.

Wellington and Uxbridge surveyed the scene.

"Where are Blücher and the damned Prussians? Our forces are shattered. One decisive blow could finish us off."

"We need more troops!" Wellington exclaimed.

"Do you want me to make some?" Uxbridge retorted.

"No, but help me hold out for the Prussians." He looked toward the heavens, "Give me night, or give me Blücher."

In the midst of this inferno Wellington rode along his shattered line, urging his troops to hold out a little longer. Uxbridge did the same, trying to rally his weary men and their horses.

The Prussian reinforcements were very slow to arrive, but had never a more welcome sight met their eyes. All was not lost yet.

"We have to hold out until the sun sets!" Nathaniel urged his weary, reluctant men on. "The Prussians are here to help. Do not give up! Victory is ours!"

Wellington shouted, "Up, Guards, and at them again!"

The Guard unit rose up from behind their protective bank of a road and poured round after round into the ranks of the French Imperial Guard. Their grenadiers then hesitated, then turned and retreated. An Allied brigade which had concealed itself suddenly appeared on the French cavalry's flank. The cavalry stopped and turned to flee.

At last Wellington waved his hat, ordering his entire line forward. The French were unable to form and after a fierce fight the remainder retreated as well.

Nathaniel made his final charge into the last stand.

It was not until the arrival of the Prussians that the scales were tipped for an Allied victory.

That morning, Lydia again made her way to the café to see if any news had been heard, and to share what little she knew with Mr. Groendyke. The sounds of gunfire first resounded around eleven in the morning, and the wounded again came through the city gate in carts and on foot. Today was different. She could feel it. Her stomach tied itself in knots, waiting for news. With each body that passed, she looked for Nathaniel's face.

Mr. Groendyke was not there that morning. Lydia waited for an hour to see if he was only late, but decided he was likely helping the wounded. Hopefully he had not received ill news of his son. She left the café, and found herself again in the thick of the efforts to help those who were making their way back from the fighting at Waterloo.

Desperate for news of Nathaniel, she did what little she could to help. She had little notion of nursing skills, but she could fetch supplies and drinks. She watched many young men, having walked all the way from the battlefield wounded, only to die when they reached the city.

She was unaccustomed to death, save that of her parents when she was a small child. It was difficult not to be angry and disillusioned by what she saw. So many dead and wounded, forever marred by a few moments' fire or the thrust of one sabre, and the fight had only begun a few hours ago. How many more would have to die before the day was done? Did these men truly understand what they were fighting for? Most were no older than she, not having had the chance to truly live yet. Still, she respected their sacrifice.

She worked in the heat for hours until she was too dizzy and tired to stand upright. She made her way back to the tiny house with the red door and red shutters. She called for a bath and prepared herself for yet another day of waiting and helping the wounded. She said prayers for Nathaniel's safety and hoped this wretched battle would end soon.

CHAPTER 14

*L*ydia had finally given up waiting, when she heard the knocker fall on the door. She anxiously opened the door to find Andrew Abbott standing before her, not Nathaniel. That could not be good. She stood staring at Andrew for a moment, searching his eyes for answers and not wanting to hear the words she knew were coming. What she saw in his eyes immediately threw her into despair –her worst fears become reality. If only she hadn't had the short glimpse of heaven.

"Is he...gone?"

Andrew hesitated, "I fear it is so. He has not yet been found. I have been searching since the battle was over, with no luck. I came to let you know. I am going back to search until I find him. I will return to help you afterwards."

Lydia wanted to be strong in that moment. It was what she had feared, what she deserved, but her heart did not believe. It refused to let go. Her throat tightened, and she found she could not speak. She felt his arms come around her and hold her tight as sobs overcame her. He eventually released his hold on her as her weeping quieted.

"I must go, but I will return soon."

"I am going with you."

"I do not think that is a good idea. Nathaniel would want you to remember him as he was. You should never know what it is like out there."

"It cannot be worse than I have imagined and seen here these few days. Please. I need to do this."

Andrew must have seen the desperation in her face, for he nodded reluctantly.

"Would you mind saddling the grey mare at the stables, while I inform Nurse where I am going?"

Once done, Lydia and Andrew rode and in silence most of the way to the battlefield. It was a slow ride, for the roads were littered with carts and the wounded and, as they drew close to the battlefield, dead bodies. Fortunately, on horseback, they were able to cut across fields.

Andrew spoke as they drew near to the farm of La Haye Sainte, the last place he had seen Nathaniel alive. "Lady Lydia, are you sure you want to continue? I have been a soldier for six years and have never seen anything so horrid as this."

"Of course I am not sure, but if he has not been found and there is still a chance... I cannot live with myself until we find him – either way."

Andrew seemed to understand. He nodded and led the way. They were forced to dismount and tie their horses to a tree. The bodies were piled everywhere, having died where they fell. There were thousands upon thousands of bodies and parts, mangled and distorted. Lydia fought back nausea. She would have perhaps been all right if she had not had to look at the faces, or smelled the stench of smoke mixed with sweat, blood and death.

She limited her search to the bodies in red tunics, but they were innumerable. She shuddered, but kept going, trying to numb her emotions. Andrew wandered off in a different direction, talking to everyone he encountered.

There were many other women out searching for their husbands, wailing when they found them. Lydia began to lose hope with each mutilated body she saw. The eyes of death were what would haunt her, she knew. Hundreds of soldiers were also out searching for the wounded in hope of finding survivors, but the conditions were impossible in the darkness. Andrew returned with some lanterns.

"No one has seen Nathaniel since the final surge. I do not know how long these lanterns will last, but we are useless without them."

"At least we know the last time he was seen alive. Does anyone know which direction he went?"

"The surge was toward the right of the chaussée. I learned that Lord Uxbridge was hit in the leg and has been taken to the surgeon at Headquarters. I am going that way to see if I can learn anything there. It is possible Nathaniel accompanied him."

Lydia carried on while Andrew sought out the makeshift hospital. She directed her search toward the right as Andrew had recommended. At times, she saw visions so horrific that tears overcame her. She had heard and read about battles, but no one could accurately put into words the carnage, or what it was like to see thousands upon thousands of dead all around you. She made it to the end of the open space near a copse of trees and sat to rest for a few moments. She would never be able to erase these visions, or the sounds that the wounded and dying were making. She wished she could either help, or that she had her own gun with unlimited shots to relieve them of the misery as they begged for her to do. She had no idea how long she had been searching. Her lantern had run out of oil, so it had to have been several hours.

She forced herself back to her feet to search some more, for what if Nathaniel were lying somewhere wounded and dying? The thought of that gave her a rush of energy. She looked back over the area she had searched, trying to maintain her bearings in the darkness. She did not know if Andrew would be able to find her again, but she kept going until the bodies at last became sparse as she reached the edge of the battlefield. There she met a few French out looking for their own survivors and asked if there were any other places where wounded had been taken.

One soldier saw her face in the breaking light of dawn, covered with dirt and streaks of tears, and must have taken pity on her. He offered her a drink and asked in broken English, "Who do you look for?"

"Colonel Fairmont of the cavalry. He wore a red tunic when last I saw him." She spoke in French to ease the soldiers understanding.

"I am not familiar with that name. The English one they call Achilles was taken to a nearby farmhouse. I do not know if this is whom you seek."

"I do not know either, but I am desperate. Can you tell me the way?" Lydia asked, trying not to get excited. That name could be anyone.

"It is over the hill, perhaps half a mile. Do you have a horse?"

She nodded. "I left it near La Haye Sainte, tied to a tree. Should I retrieve her?"

"Yes, it will be a long way back for you."

After retrieving the mare, she had difficulty mounting her because of her exhaustion.

"Let me help you." She turned to find Andrew standing behind her.

"Oh, thank God. I did not know if I would see you again. Did you find him?"

Andrew shook his head. "And no one seems to know. The good news is that no one saw him go down either."

"A French soldier told me they took the one they call Achilles to a nearby farmhouse. I was about to go there now."

"By Jove, that's Nathaniel! That is what they call him!" He excitedly threw her up into the saddle and mounted his own horse.

"Lead the way!"

Lydia and Andrew could not get to the small farmhouse fast enough. They went as fast as possible, dodging bodies, hedges, and trees. By the time they reached the farm, Lydia's stomach was in knots. She had no idea what they would find when they went inside. What if the French soldier had been wrong? Andrew helped her dismount but stopped her before they went into the house.

"Let me go in first. He might not even be here."

Lydia did not want to wait, but she knew Andrew was right. She nodded and stood by the door.

She grew impatient after she had waited several minutes. She began to pace back and forth, fearing the worst. When Andrew finally came back outside he looked like he had seen a ghost.

"Is it him?"

Andrew nodded but remained silent.

"I am going inside." Andrew grabbed her arm and pulled her back as she made for the door.

"Lydia, wait." She stopped and looked at Andrew. "He is in poor shape...he's dying."

Lydia did not need to hear any more. She tore herself from Andrew's hold and ran into the house. She was not prepared for what she saw. Several wounded soldiers were lying all over the tiny parlour, bandaged and bleeding. She looked from body to body, frantically searching for him. A wrinkled old woman finally told her the one she looked for was in another room, pointing and nodding her head towards a bedroom off the parlour. Lydia fixed her attention on making her way to that door. When she entered the room, Andrew had caught up with her.

Nathaniel was unrecognizable. Half of his face was bandaged, the other half covered with dirt and blood. A bandage covered part of his arm where his hand used to be. His shirt had been torn from his body, and a doctor was holding pressure to a stomach wound that would not stop bleeding. His body was shaking and he was groaning in agony. When she recovered herself, she went over to his side and took his right hand. His batman, Ajax, had moved out of the way to allow her by Nathaniel's side.

"Nathaniel. It is Lydia. I am here, my love."

He struggled to open his right eye and turned his head slightly toward her. He tried to speak but the effort was too great.

"Shh. Do not try to speak. I am here now."

A tear fell from his eye. Lydia struggled to control her emotions.

Nathaniel's breathing became more laboured and the doctor began urging her in French to leave.

"He has lost too much blood for me to save. I gave him a large dose of medicine. Let him die in peace. This is no place for a lady." The doctor handed over the job of holding Nathaniel's bandage and went on to find a patient he could save.

Lydia did not know what to do. She did not want to leave his side, but the doctor clearly felt her presence was making Nathaniel suffer. Andrew gently began leading her toward the door. She shook her head. Before she let go of his hand, Nathaniel managed to say, "I am sorry." His mouth was dry and she held a drink of brandy to his lips. "Tell....Amelia."

She bent over and gently kissed him. She whispered, "I will. I will tell her you love her...and I love you," into his ear and let herself be pulled away.

She held herself together until they were outside the house.

Andrew tried to hug her, but she pushed him away.

"Go be with him, so he does not have to die alone."

"He would not want me to leave you," Andrew protested.

"I need to be alone. I can find my way back. I need to be with our little girl. Go. He needs you."

Andrew obviously did not wish to leave her in this state, but he visibly struggled with what was best.

"Go! Please!" She walked over and tried to mount her horse. Andrew held his hands for her, and then squeezed her hand before turning away.

She turned and watched Andrew walk back to the house before urging the horse forward. She stopped several times, wanting to go back and be with Nathaniel, but talked herself into continuing, not wanting to worsen his suffering. Leaving Nathaniel dying in pain was the hardest thing she had had to do, next to leaving her infant daughter in someone else's care.

She rode on for several miles, barely able to see through her tears. She needed to be able to control herself before telling Amelia that the father she just met had already been taken from her. She did not know how she would be able to go on, herself.

Watching Lydia ride off, Andrew had second thoughts. He knew in his heart that Nathaniel would want him to help her, not wait hopelessly for him to die. He walked back in to find Ajax crying over his master's immobile body.

Andrew sucked in his breath. "Is it finished then?"

Ajax nodded without looking up, too heartbroken to speak.

Andrew walked over and put his arm on Nathaniel, still warm, unable to believe.

Ajax handed him Nathaniel's ring which he had removed from Nathaniel's hand.

"Thank you, I will return this to his father. Will you see that his body is returned to the Duke? I must look after Lady Fairmont. It was his wish."

"Of course, Major. I would do nothing less for my master."

Andrew gave Nathaniel a final salute then turned on his heel to go after Lydia.

CHAPTER 15

*L*ydia felt as though she had been kicked in the chest. She could not stop the unbearable pain. She even felt guilty for having it. What right did she have to feel this way after only one week of marriage? But she did. She ached inside, not only for herself but for their precious daughter, who would never truly know her father. She was grateful for the short acquaintance they had made, and hoped Amelia would be able to cherish that when she grew older. Lydia knew that she held on to her few memories of her parents and treasured them more than anything. She could not bring herself to regret the events leading up to the battle. She could not help but feel that Nathaniel had felt some affection for her. She would have to hold onto that to get her through the anguish.

She struggled to stay atop her horse as she negotiated her way back to Brussels. By that point, she was exhausted and numb, sure the last hours had to be a horrid nightmare she could not wake up from. It was late in the morning when she finally arrived at the Rue de Madeleine, and was grateful to find that Nurse and Amelia were out. She was not sure how to face them yet. The housekeeper saw the blood and mud-stained state she was in, and immediately helped her to wash, change and crawl into bed.

It was dark by the time Lydia stirred. She felt her tiny daughter's body curled up next to her. There was a small amount of light in the room from a flickering taper by her bedside. She raised her head to see Nurse sleeping in a chair beside her bed. She began to remember what had occurred that day and pulled Amelia into her arms and held her tight as warm tears rolled down her face again. Would it ever stop hurting?

What was she to do now? Nathaniel had assured her that she and Amelia would be provided for, should something happen to him. Should she go back to England to his family? The thought of returning without him was unbearable to her. She did not wish for Amelia to be raised under the umbrella of her parents' sins. She was also uncertain of their acceptance by the Duke and Duchess. Perhaps one day she might be able to face England again, but it held no happy memories for her and no immediate desire to return.

No, she must make a new life for her and her daughter. She could proceed with her original plan now that she did not have to worry about money. If that failed, she could always consider America. Even though Britain had lost the war with them, Nathaniel seemed to feel it was an acceptable place for them. Perhaps Major Abbott would help her if she changed her mind.

The decision made, Lydia felt a sense of urgency to leave. She did not want any reminders of this battle around her. She picked her daughter up and carried her back to her own bed and tucked her in. She went back in and woke Nurse so she could be comfortable in her own bed. That done, Lydia packed, determined to leave first thing in the morning. She dressed in her darkest, most drab gown, which would have to do until she could procure proper mourning attire. She held each of the new dresses she never had the chance to wear in her hands, letting the beautifully coloured fabrics fall through her fingers, and sighed with regret. How different she had felt only a few days ago. She could not believe he was never coming back. She came to the ball gown she had worn that last magical night with Nathaniel and could not imagine going on without him. It could not be real. She would like nothing more than to scream in anger and vent her frustrations. She sat on the bed and cried. But it would do Amelia no good for her to be angry—or become a watering pot. She rose to finish with her things and went to the kitchen to make herself some tea. She realized she had not eaten and had barely had anything to drink for the past two days.

She passed through the parlour on her way to the kitchen and nearly stumbled over Major Abbott sleeping on the floor, still in his muddy and bloody uniform. She had to stop a scream from escaping her lips. She did not wish to wake him and tiptoed around him.

"Lady Lydia?"

She heard him call sleepily after her. "I did not mean to wake you, Major Abbott. I did not realize you were there."

"No, forgive me for sleeping on the floor, I was afraid to touch the furniture in my dirtied state. When I arrived, you were asleep, so I decided to wait for you to awaken."

Lydia sobered. She dreaded asking the question she knew the answer to. "Is it over, then?"

Andrew nodded. "His batman is having his body sent back to England. I have already written to inform the Duke. I know it is early yet, but I will escort you when you are ready to return."

Lydia shook her head. "I am not going back."

"Pardon? Where will you go? Surely you do not mean to stay here?"

"No. The reason I came to Brussels was only to ask for help in setting up a new home in France. I think it best, given my current situation, to continue with that plan."

"I do not understand. You are now Lady Fairmont. You will be accepted everywhere."

"But what of Amelia?" She could see the uncertainty on Andrew's face. "Precisely. If I were certain that the Duke and Duchess would accept their granddaughter, I might consider returning. But I cannot, therefore I will make a happy home for the two of us. It will not be the same without Nathaniel, but I will do the best I can to give my daughter the love that I did not have away from Society's judgements."

"I cannot change your mind?"

Lydia shook her head.

"Then I will see you to where you wish to go."

"That is most kind of you, Major, but I cannot impose on you in such a fashion. We journeyed here despite our circumstances. I am certain that now, with funds, we will arrive at our destination without incident."

"Forgive me for saying so, but that is an ignorant assumption. It will be extremely difficult to find passage at this time. Besides that, I promised your husband I would look after you. Amelia is now my god-daughter."

Lydia raised her head up in surprise. Andrew pulled the Will from his pocket and handed it to Lydia. As she read through, she covered her mouth with her hand to muffle the sounds of astonishment she was making. "Dear God, he thought of everything."

"He cared for both of you."

Lydia had to turn to hide more tears. Would they never dry up? She wanted to be strong for her daughter's sake.

"I must leave you now to see to preparations. I am not sure how long it will take me to procure leave and transportation."

"Amelia has a pony and I have a horse we can use."

"What of your Nurse?"

Lydia shook her head.

"I will return as soon as I am able."

Lydia reached out to Andrew and gave his hand a squeeze of thanks. He turned quickly and left.

Lydia headed into the kitchen after Major Abbott was gone. She placed the kettle on the stove, and sat staring at the wall. She tried to think of anything other than Nathaniel. Even recalling the happy times from years ago, or this week, of him playing with his daughter, caused her throat to tighten. Thank God she had Amelia to live for. She thought of all of the other wives she saw looking for their loved ones on the battlefield. She would never forget their screams and wails of anguish. She was not the only one who must endure this, but most of them would not be left in such comfortable circumstances as she had been. How strange it was to think of comfort at a time such as this. Part of her felt a tug at her heart to return to England to help the misfortunate of the war, and perhaps one day she would do that. She needed time away, however, to grieve and to simply be with her daughter. How could one week change her feelings so much? Before, she had been content to be alone. Now, her heart was in agony, in too much pain to be dead.

The kettle began to billow and she jumped up to turn it off. She made her cup of tea and then settled on the sofa to enjoy her drink. The one thing she knew already – she was going to have to keep herself occupied. The hardest moments were when she was alone to think.

She was soon awakened by the cook and housekeeper arriving to start their day. She decided to go on and begin packing Amelia's belongings; she wanted to be ready whenever Major Abbott arrived. She prayed that it would not be long.

Andrew left Lydia's house and headed to the Brussels headquarters. Many had already made their way back from Waterloo, and the staff was taking reports, trying to determine survivors, wounded, and dead. The war was over, but there was much work yet to be done. The dead must be buried, and Napoleon must be dealt with. He knew his commander would likely be off to Paris soon. As much as he hated asking for leave, he could meet up with him in the city.

Andrew approached one of the other staff members. "How is he right now?" referring to the Duke of Wellington.

"Sober. We lost too many great men—friends."

Andrew nodded. "I must ask him for leave. I need to escort Lady Fairmont."

The officer whistled through his teeth. "Best go on and ask. There will not be any good time the next few days, anyhow."

"True. He is not with anyone at the moment?"

"Surprisingly, no. He just returned from the infirmary."

Andrew knocked on the Duke's door.

"Enter." The Duke was sitting at a table scrawling his *Waterloo Dispatch* to Lord Bathurst in England.

"Ah, Abbott. There you are. Are you hiding any wounds? You look untouched."

"Only a few scratches, sir."

"You and I are of the few." Both thought sadly of their dear friend Colonel Gordon who had passed away during the night.

"Do you leave me now, or do you go on to Paris?"

"I need to leave you for a while, sir. I need to escort Lady Fairmont, if possible."

The Duke raised an eyebrow and began to ask a question, but they were interrupted. The Duke stood and turned toward Andrew and said, "Do what you must, of course. Send word of your intentions when you know them." He nodded his dismissal and turned toward the messenger.

That had been easier than Andrew had thought it would be. He went to his quarters and packed up his belongings. He then set out about the more difficult task of finding transportation to Paris. He was unsure where Lydia meant to settle, but it would be easier to find accommodation from the capital. People had been paying inordinate amounts for horses while trying to escape Brussels, and with the number of horses killed in action, he had no idea how he would be able to purchase more. He walked along the Rue Royale searching for any mode of transport to hire. It seemed as though every cart and carriage was being used to carry the wounded and dead. There were no horses to be had in any part of Brussels either. He himself was down to his last horse, having had two of his stock shot out from under him on the battlefield. It was much the same for everyone. He made his way back to Headquarters to see if any of the staff had any ideas. Before he walked through the door, it occurred to him that Nathaniel might have some spare, although it was unlikely. Though the last time he had seen Nathaniel, he was still atop Salty.

He went through the door and enquired of the staff once again. It would not be necessary to seek out Nathaniel's cattle, for another internal staff member was happy to lend one of his older nags to the cause. Andrew was much obliged and gathered his belongings, bidding his staff mates farewell.

Leading the nag to Lydia's house, he thanked the heavens for his luck. He did not look forward to leading everyone to Paris on horseback, but there would be no other options for some time. He would need to undertake this errand and be back to Wellington as soon as possible. He deposited the horses at the stables, rubbed them down and gave them some oats for the long journey ahead.

CHAPTER 16

*W*hen Nurse and Amelia made their way into the parlour the next morning, Lydia knew she had to tell her daughter. She dreaded it more than anything she had ever faced. Her daughter ran to her for a hug, and she held her so tight that Amelia complained. Lydia looked up at her nurse, gazing at her knowingly, and tears began to fall from both their eyes. Lydia sucked in a succession of sobs, trying to hold back. She did not want to grieve in front of Amelia.

"What is the matter, Mama?"

Children were too perceptive. She sat on the sofa, still holding her daughter. She looked at her sweet child, the mirror image of her father, and took a deep breath.

"Amelia, you know that your papa had to go fight in the war?"

"Yes, he is the fiewcest, bwavest soldier there is," she said proudly. "The dook told me so."

"Did he? Well, there can be no doubt then."

Lydia did not know if she could do this. How would a five-year-old handle the news?

"Amelia?"

"Yes, Mama?"

"Your papa was hurt very badly during the battle yesterday."

"Oh, dear," she said, and worry creased her face. "Can I see him? I can kiss his huwts and make them better."

Lydia's heart gave a lurch. "I'm afraid not, sweetheart. Papa's hurts were too severe. Even the doctor could not make them better."

"Did he go to live with the angels then?" she asked innocently.

"Yes, I am afraid he did."

"Then at least we can see him again. That's what Nuwse says. If I am very good, I will live with the angels one day."

She let out a breath of relief. She had not thought a young child would understand so much. She was grateful to Nurse for the way she had brought up Amelia so far.

"I am sad, Mama."

"I am, too, my love. I miss him already."

"How long will it be until we get to live with the angels?"

"Nobody knows. But at least we have that to look forward to one day."

Amelia nodded. She saw her kitten from across the floor and chose to run after him. Lydia went to her room. She could not keep herself composed. She wished she had the understanding of her daughter, but all she felt was confusion and pain. She threw herself on the bed and allowed herself to lose control.

Lydia could barely remember the trip from Brussels to Paris. At times she felt her head was in a fog and she only managed to go through the motions. At other times, she was so tired she could barely sit on her horse. She would be eternally grateful to Major Abbott, for he took Amelia up on his horse with him the entire way. He, too, was discovering a five-year-old girl was a never-ending source of questions and observations. They had been obliged to travel to Paris without a carriage, but whenever she offered to take Amelia, he would refuse and state he enjoyed the time becoming acquainted with his god-daughter.

Nurse was a nervous wreck, and held on to her horse for dear life. Major Abbott had found an old, worn-out nag for her, but she was still convinced she would be thrown, or fall off, and die. Not only did Major Abbott entertain Amelia and hold her and her kitten when she slept, but he guided Nurse and her horse, soothing the old lady's nerves and distracting her with endless conversation. He had to be grieving as much as Lydia, but she could not have managed without him. She followed quietly behind, leading Amelia's pony which was packed down with luggage. She was left to her own thoughts for the most part. She could cry silently to herself and not have to answer anyone.

They arrived in Paris travel-worn and dirty. As they rode up to the mews behind the hotel, Lydia did not know if she would be able to sit or walk for days after being in the saddle for so long. She dismounted gingerly and went to Major Abbott to relieve him of Amelia, who was sleeping.

Unfortunately, Major Abbott had forgotten about *Chaton*, who had been sleeping cosily inside his coat pocket. The kitten jumped when Major Abbott began to dismount. He flung his arms out in attempt to catch the small creature, but missed. The kitten landed on the horse's hind quarters, and the horse reared when her claws dug into his flesh. Major Abbott had not the luxury of time to remove his boot from the stirrup, and was tossed ungracefully into a puddle.

Lydia watched the scene like it was a farce on the stage. She was helpless to act with her sleeping daughter in her arms. She stood with her mouth gaping, unsure of what to do. Major Abbott appeared to be unharmed, yet he lay there covered in mud. Nurse still clung to her horse for dear life, waiting for someone to help her dismount. Nurse would be fine for a moment longer. Lydia walked over to Major Abbott to see if he was harmed. She nudged him with her foot and he burst out laughing.

"Major Abbott?" she asked cautiously.

"I am all right. Forgive me for laughing. This was all the day wanted to be complete."

Lydia agreed and could no longer hold back her own laughter. Once they began, they could not seem to stop.

Nurse began to cry, and Major Abbott hopped out of the puddle to assist her. When she'd got down from the horse, she rang a peal over the both of them for laughing hysterically while she suffered.

This did nothing more than cause more hysteria. Nurse relieved Lydia of Amelia and stomped off into the hotel with a loud *humph*.

"Thank you. I needed that," Lydia said with a hiccough, and giggled.

"You are very welcome. Glad to be of service, my lady," he said with a large grin and a royal bow.

Major Abbott procured them accommodation along the Seine River, near the new British Embassy across from the Champs Élysées. There they remained for a few days while Lydia obtained some proper mourning attire, and Major Abbott searched and asked around about hiring cottages in the south.

One morning over *crêpes* and *chocolát*, he joined them to ask her for more guidance in his search.

"What do you remember about the cottage and village where you stayed with your parents?"

"I do not remember the name of the village. I know it was along a river, and the hills were covered with vineyards." Lydia smiled, recalling the happy times with her parents.

"You know nothing other than this was south of Paris? You have essentially described most of France."

"I will know it when we see it?" She smiled sheepishly, knowing she was searching for a needle in a haystack.

Andrew stared at her blankly.

"Of course, I do not expect you to escort us all over France. I believe I would like to start along the river in the Loire Valley. I saw a painting of a large château once and I remember seeing it as a child. I cannot believe the village would be too far from there."

"That does narrow it down. Do you remember the name?"

"Chambord, I believe it was."

"I know of it. We passed near there on our march north. I will see about procuring transportation and ask about accommodation there."

"I realize the place may no longer exist as I remember it. But for now, I need to try. It was a happy time for me and I need to find that again." At least she had her daughter now, and this was a dream she had fought for years to achieve. She would have to be content with that.

Lydia loved Paris, but needed the peace of the country for now. When she saw a couple arguing, she was so angry she had wanted to throw something at them and yell ungracefully for them to appreciate what they had before it was too late. She knew then she needed to get away.

She looked out over the countryside as they rolled south away from the city. She inhaled a deep breath and felt herself relax. She still could not believe what had happened during the past month. It did not seem real. She had been alternating between anger and weeping to the point where she was growing numb. Her gaze fell to Amelia, napping on Nurse's lap, then to the ring Nathaniel had given her. She watched Major Abbott trot along beside the carriage, a reminder that it was all too real.

She laughed as she spied the basket Major Abbott had purchased for the kitten. He had become wise since their first trip. He had filled it with treats and yarn for the cat to play with. This had the unforeseen consequence of eternally endearing the cat to him. As soon as she saw him, *Chaton* would run to him and rub herself all over his ankles.

Over the next two days, they passed through beautiful tall birch and evergreen forests, which would suddenly open up onto a vast field or vineyard. Lydia was relieved to be beginning again, away from the reminders of her past, and where she would have the freedom to be with her daughter openly.

After two long days of travel, they arrived in Orleáns. It was not as far as she wanted to go, but Major Abbott felt it would be the best place to start her search for a home, having had little luck in Paris. Lydia stepped out of the carriage and felt a sense of peace wash over her. This was right. It might not be permanent, but it was right for now. She had no other choice but to start again, and this was on her own terms. They were high on a hill, and she stepped out a few feet and looked around the valley below her. The sun had cast a golden hue down over the landscape, accentuating the natural beauty of the vineyard-covered hills. The beauty stole her breath.

They were shown into their accommodation for the night, and Lydia left Major Abbott while he enquired after their supper and about where to begin looking for cottages. They made their way to their rooms and the view was beyond words. She felt she might like to stay here forever. Her room looked out over the river and they were surrounded by forests or farms as far as the eye could see.

After they had washed and rested, Major Abbott knocked on their door to lead them to supper. A table had been set out on the terrace overlooking the river. A soft summer breeze caressed her skin and brought the fresh scent of summer with it. Lydia knew she could be happy here.

"Have you any news on where to begin our search? I do not wish to detain you any longer. I am certain we can manage from here."

"I appreciate that, but I would prefer to see you situated. I heard from the owner that there is a possible place about twenty miles west of here."

"Could we be so fortunate?" Lydia's eyes brightened as she took a sip of the most delectable wine she had ever tasted.

"It sounded as if the cottage was on a larger manorial estate. Perhaps a dower house? The property was only recently vacated. He was not certain the owner would wish to hire it out, but he said it was worth the trip if only to see the Châteaux."

"I am willing to give it a try."

Major Abbott took a bite of some fresh bread and cheese, and grunted in appreciation. "I might have to beg you to take your time looking. I think I could stay here for the food alone."

She laughed at his ungentlemanly, honest gestures. "The food, the wine, the view, I am thankful my childhood memories did not deceive me. I am quite in love with this area at the moment."

They ate in silent appreciation for several minutes before he spoke again.

"Lady Lydia, I hope you find what you are looking for here. I will return and visit my god-daughter from time to time, as well."

"That is kind of you. I know Amelia will enjoy that."

"I do not want you to feel as if you were abandoned either. I confess, I am not sure how my aunt and uncle will feel about the marriage, but I hope in time they will want to know their grand-daughter."

Lydia remained silent. She expected the worst from the Duke and Duchess with regard to her and her daughter. If they chose not to publicly accept her, there would be no chance for Amelia.

"She is his legacy," Andrew defended, reading her thoughts.

"That is not the same as an heir. That would be entirely different."

"I will always be available to help. You only have to ask." He looked so sincere and genuine that her heart was touched.

"I know that. Thank you. You have done so much. I do not know what I would have done without your help." She reached over and gave his hands a squeeze, and had to leave before she became a watering pot again. Would it never stop?

The next morning they set out early for the cottage. Lydia had no idea what to expect. She was trying to be content with being away from her uncle, and also having Amelia to herself. This situation would be unbearable without her. Having the opportunity to see everything through a child's eyes was enlightening. She had been an only child, and had a few memories of happiness with her parents before they died, but afterwards, when she was sent to live with her aunt and uncle, she had known only loneliness. A child raised in an adult's world.

"Look, Mama! Look! Look! Cindewella's castle!" Amelia was so excited, Lydia thought she might fall out of the carriage. Lydia snapped from her mental wanderings and looked at the Château before them and smiled.

"That is the Château I remember as a girl," she exclaimed. "I was about your age when I came here with my parents. Surely this is not the one with the cottage, Major Abbott?"

"I do not believe so. I do not think we are far away now, however."

They all stared out at the magnificent edifice dreamily. It was impossible to not be swept away by something so grand. They continued on, but Lydia wanted to return to visit again another day. It was a few more miles before they pulled into the gates of the manor. It was not a grand château; in fact, it reminded her more of an English country house. The three-storeyed walls were covered in ivy over a white stone, and the garden was brilliantly coloured in full bloom.

As they pulled to the front of the drive, Lydia felt strange about intruding upon a stranger and asking about their cottage.

Andrew must have sensed the hesitation on her face. "I will do all of the talking. Perhaps you should stay in the carriage while I enquire?"

"I think I would prefer that. If the family is away, will you ask if we may have a look around?"

"Certainly."

It was not long before Andrew returned. "The owner is out on the estate. The steward expects him to return soon and offered for us to make ourselves comfortable. Would you like to go inside?"

"I believe I would like to walk around for now."

"Mama, I'm hungwy." Amelia spoke.

"Yes, of course. Do you think they would mind?"

"I will take Amelia and Nurse in. Go on and walk around," Andrew offered.

"Thank you, Major Abbott."

Lydia heard him say to Nurse as they walked away, "I suppose it is time you learned French, Madame."

"Now why would I want to do that?"

"*Pour charmer vos nombreux prétendants, bien sûr*," Andrew said with a devastating smile.

"Now why do I think you said something you oughtn't have?"

He only laughed and followed her into the house.

Lydia wandered around the gardens and saw no sign of a cottage. She saw a path through some trees and followed it curiously. She hoped she was not exceeding her welcome. The path wound around and broke through some trees. She had not thought there could be any sight more glorious than she had already witnessed, but she was wrong. She gaped in astonishment at the scene before her.

"It is incredible, no?" A deep voice said from behind her.

Lydia jumped. She had not realized she was not alone. "Forgive me. I walked too far."

"There is nothing to forgive, *mademoiselle*. You are most welcome to Maison Belle Vue."

"Indeed." It was a beautiful view. "Are you the owner?"

He nodded, "Yves Clement at your service." He bowed regally.

"Madame Fairmont." She held out her hand, which he took and graced with an elegant kiss.

"What brings you to this house?"

She looked down and tried to contain her flush. "We were told you might have a cottage available to rent."

"Ah. My *mère* recently passed away. You must refer to this."

"I am terribly sorry for your loss."

"You too have suffered a recent loss?" He indicated her mourning attire.

"Yes, my husband was killed in the recent battle at Waterloo."

"So young. Please accept my condolences. Would you like to see the house? It is nearby."

"If it would not trouble you terribly. My daughter and nurse are at the house with our cousin."

"I shall show you now, and if you are pleased, you may show it to them."

He led her on down the path and around a curve, to where the most charming cottage sat overlooking the river. It had a better view than the manor house. She gasped when she saw it.

He smiled. "I will never tire of the view myself. Would you like to see inside?"

"Yes, please, *monsieur.*"

The cottage was perfect. It was small, but large enough for the three of them. At the back was a lovely garden where Amelia could run and play. There was even a large wooden swing tied to a tree.

"Are you sure you would not mind us living here?"

"You would be most welcome. It is sitting empty and of use to anyone at the moment. Shall we return to the house to retrieve the others?" He held out his arm with a twinkle in his eye. She returned his smile and took the offered escort.

At this point, Andrew wished he had a batman, a groom, anybody or anyone to help, whom he could leave to watch over them until he could return. He hated leaving Nathaniel's grieving widow behind, but he had his duty to Wellington and England as well. But Lady Lydia had been adamant; she did not wish for him to stay. He understood her sentiments, for he also wanted some time alone to grieve. However, he had become used to losing people, if that were possible. It came with his occupation.

Something nagged at his conscience that he should not leave a young, beautiful widow alone with only her small child and nurse. Some protection that would be. The owner of the manor seemed to be fond of them—perhaps too fond—but that would be Lydia's business when she was out of mourning.

He rode as fast as he could to Paris. He was thinking about everything he still needed to take care of with regard to Nathaniel. He patted his jacket pocket and felt Nathaniel's ring, and then he remembered the letter he had forgotten to post to his uncle. Andrew could not believe he could have forgotten such a thing. He hated the thought that his aunt and uncle had probably heard of Nathaniel's death from someone else. He let out an exasperated sigh. It could not be helped. He had been in haste, and at least he had helped Lady Lydia find her way to where she wanted to be.

CHAPTER 17

The Duke of Loring paced around his study. The family had just returned from Scotland, where Beatrice had married Lord Vernon. They were headed to the Continent soon for their honeymoon. One problem was resolved, at least.

He had hoped upon his return to London he would find an errant letter from Nathaniel, or some positive word from the investigators he had sent to look for his son, but there was little news to be had. He would have to go to Brussels himself. Then again, he thought, perhaps he should begin in Paris with Wellington and his staff. His investigators said they had done an exhaustive search—to include every known hospital and posting house— of Waterloo and Brussels. But there was no sign of Nathaniel.

There were officers of lesser rank who had been returned to England for burial. Things simply did not add up. He had even spoken to the Lords Uxbridge and Somerset, who had been in direct command of Nathaniel's regiment, and neither could explain what could have happened to his son or his batman, Ajax. They had seen him at the very last moment of the battle.

He had waited long enough. He must go and look himself.

The Duchess soon found her way to the study, anxious to see if there was any word.

"Is there any news?"

He shook his hand, "I am afraid not."

"We are no better off than we were before we left for Scotland."

"There is no word of his death, at least."

"What do we do now?"

The Duke raised his eyebrows at her use of 'we'. "There is nothing to do but for me to go and look for myself."

"Then I shall come with you. When do we leave?"

The Duke had to stop himself from saying something tactless. He had no idea how his wife thought she would be of any use to him whatsoever. She had been more reserved since leaving Scotland, but that did not mean she would not be a nuisance while he was searching for Nathaniel. There would be little luxury to this trip, and he did not mean to accommodate her idea of roughing it.

"Wilhelmina, I do not think it prudent for you to accompany me. There will be nothing pleasant about this journey, and I cannot be certain of what we will find. The country has been ravaged by the war and there may be times we are forced to sleep in less than desirous conditions."

"I understand."

"I am glad you are able to see reason. I do appreciate your wanting to help."

"No, Robert, I understand the conditions may not be pleasant, but I do not wish to remain here alone."

"Wilhelmina..." He took a steadying breath. This was not the time to get angry or lose patience with her. She might act like the veriest ninny at times, but he knew seeing Beatrice wed, yet not knowing whether her son was alive or dead, had been torture for her too. "I will not be able to attend to your needs. We cannot take an entourage with us on this occasion. Are you prepared to travel without a maid?"

She flinched slightly but nodded. "If I must."

"There will be no place for hysterics; no vinaigrette, no smelling salts."

She stiffened, but said nothing.

He stared at her and saw she was in earnest. "Very well. Have your things packed, and pack lightly, for we will leave at daybreak. I have already ordered the yacht to be ready to leave tomorrow. And Wilhelmina," he called after her as she was leaving the study.

"Yes, Robert?"

"Make sure to pack some riding habits. We may be obliged to do a fair amount of riding." He saw her hesitate, knowing that she normally avoided riding at all costs, but she said, "Very well, Robert," and continued on her way.

Had the situation not been so dire, he would have laughed. The thought of seeing his duchess on a horse again would be humorous; almost like old times. He sighed. How he wished he could have his old Wilhelmina back. He had no intention of travelling with her without a maid, but it was a good measure of how much she must want to go, that she would do without. He shook his head; he was sure he would live to regret this, but he had arrangements to make and no time to worry about her comforts now.

Nathaniel could not get his eyes to open. In fact, he had not felt this way since...bloody hell, someone must have given him laudanum! And a great deal of it. He could hear people speaking around him in— what was that, French? Dutch? Walloon? He tried to focus on their words, but his head was spinning and he felt confused. Had he been taken prisoner? No, please do not let it be that.

Morts. Dead. *Enterrer.* Bury him. *Anglais.* England.

He wondered who had died. And he wondered why he could not open his eyes. He tried to move and felt a sharp pain in his side. He tried to move his arm, but that did not feel right either. What was going on? He searched his mind, trying to recall, but could not seem to remember what had happened. He finally managed to move a little, but the pain was so severe a groan escaped him.

"My lord? Was that you?"

Nathaniel knew that voice, but when he opened his mouth to speak he could not get the words to come out. He struggled, but his throat was too dry and his tongue was stuck to the roof of his mouth.

"Here, my lord, take a drink." The familiar voice held a drink to his lips, which felt like an oasis in the desert. He still could not see.

"Ajax."

"We…we thought you were dead, my lord."

"What happened?"

"Do you remember anything?'

Nathaniel tried to concentrate, but his head ached like the devil.

"No, but I feel like I've been drugged."

"Aye. The French surgeon dosed you fair heavy. Said there was nothing more he could do for you and thought he would ease your suffering."

"I feel as though he about did for me."

"You took some bad hits during the last charge. Your hand was shot off, you were run through by a sword, and I am not sure the extent of injury to your head. I have been gone for hours, making your arrangements, and it is glad I am to find you breathing instead of placing you in a wooden box."

Nathaniel listened to his batman, trying to process everything he said. Remembrance began to occur slowly, and in pieces. Now he knew why his arm felt strange and why his side hurt; he hoped he could see something when the bandage was removed.

"Salty?"

"Gone, my lord. Shot out from under you. That was how they took advantage of you." Ajax paused to let Nathaniel absorb the news. "I had best send for the doctor. He will not believe me until he sees you. They have cleared the other wounded out of this old farmhouse. They were kind enough to let me leave you here until, well, I returned for you. I will be back after I fetch the sawbones."

Nathaniel lay there in the darkness, still groggy and attempting to assimilate everything Ajax had said. He began to put together the last few days. The battle, the wedding…

Oh, God. Lydia. Amelia. They must think I am dead.

Pain surged through the place where Nathaniel thought he had a heart. He had wondered before the last week if it no longer existed. The realization that Lydia was gone with his daughter, and without him, made the pain from his battle wounds seem insignificant. He had to recover and find them. Perhaps Ajax knew where they were. He reminded himself to ask Ajax when he returned. He was too exhausted to remain conscious for long and allowed a deep sleep to overtake him.

"Sacré bleu! Impossible!" the French doctor exclaimed. "He was dead for certain."

"I thought so as well, sir. But he was awake and talking to me."

The doctor went closer to Nathaniel and saw that he was breathing. *"Je n'en croix pas mes yeux!"* You could not have convinced me if I had not seen it with my own eyes! *C'est un miracle!"* He crossed himself violently in accordance with his words.

"What shall we do now, Doctor? Should I try to move him to Brussels?"

"Non! He is much too weak to be moved. I still am not convinced he will survive. I will speak with the old lady and make arrangements."

Ajax was taken aback by the doctor's words. He looked around him and could not imagine remaining here to take care of his master. "How...how long do you think we will be here, Doctor?"

"I am not knowing. We still have to fear the fever."

Nathaniel began to stir. "Ajax?"

"Yes, my lord?"

"Where is Lydia? Where is Amelia? Have they left?"

"Major Abbott left to see them safe, my lord. I presume they returned to England."

Nathaniel let out an irritated sigh. "We must send word to them. I do not want her to think..."

"Yes, my lord, I will see to it at once. There are still soldiers nearby, attending to the dead."

"*Impossible!*" someone cried in an astonished tone.

"Who is there?" Nathaniel asked.

"The doctor." Ajax chuckled. "With a gaping jaw!"

"Good." Nathaniel turned toward where he heard the doctor, "Sir, how long till I can leave? And when can you remove these bandages from my head?"

"Your wounds are very serious, sir. Many months."

"I do not have months, sir. What is wrong with my head?"

The doctor hesitated, not wanting to answer.

"Sir? Ajax? Someone tell me!"

"A shell exploded near your head, sir. I do not know if you will be able to see again," Ajax answered.

Nathaniel sucked his breath in. It was one thing to deal with a sabre wound and losing a hand, it was another thing entirely to realize you would be blind— never to see again.

The doctor spoke. "You may have sight in the eye that was not damaged, but we will not know until we remove the bandages. It is too soon to take them off. The longer you keep the eyes covered, the better your chance will be. I will speak to the old woman about keeping you here for now."

Nathaniel was speechless. Blind? Eternal darkness? How fitting. He'd had a small glimpse of heaven, and he would never be able to see her – either of them – again. Perhaps they would be better off without him. No! He would not allow himself to feel that way. He would see again. He would.

CHAPTER 18

*N*athaniel could see nothing, but he could feel that he was not alone.

"Is someone there?"

An older lady's voice answered, *"Non Anglais."*

"Parlez-vous français?"

"Oui. I have some food for you. Shall I help you eat? Your man is resting."

Nathaniel agreed. He did not know if he would ever become used to being fed. There had to be a way he could feed himself without appearing as if he had served himself at the pig trough. She held a spoon to his mouth. He had learned not to flinch every time someone touched him. It was still difficult.

"Very good," he praised. "You are a talented cook."

"Flatterer. It was the same with my Joseph."

He smiled. He could just imagine her blushing and waving his comment away with her hand. He could not remember a female of his acquaintance who did not like to be appreciated.

"How long have I been here, *madame?"*

"Two weeks, I believe. I lose count. You sleep much."

"Are the soldiers still here?

"*Oui*. They are still tending to the bodies. Such a terrible loss."

Nathaniel paused.

"Keep eating. You need good food to be strong. Do you have a family to return to?"

"*Oui*."

"The beautiful lady; she is your wife?"

He nodded and winced from the pain. "We have a small daughter. She is beautiful as well."

"We must feed you more. You will be better faster. Now eat."

Mutton stew was not his favourite, but a soldier knew not to be fastidious. He was grateful to have been brought to a place where he was cared for. He doubted he would receive as much attention at the army infirmary.

"Is Joseph your husband or your son?"

"He was my husband. He passed away five years ago. My son, he was lost in battle."

"My sympathies."

She was silent. He cursed his stupidity. He should not have brought the subject up. *Another gift you took for granted when you could see was the ability to read people.* If he could have seen, he would have known they were alone. He would ensure that Ajax gave her money, or send his batman to the market to buy food. He imagined a widowed, elderly lady did not have much. He would not be a financial burden as well as a physical one.

"Do you have help with the farm?"

"*Oui*. I have men who come help for the day. The farm is not so big any more. I sold most of it when I lost Joseph."

He finished the mutton stew, as well as a delicious berry pie with fresh cream. He could certainly become accustomed to having a full belly. That was a rarity in army life at times.

"Thank you, *madame*."

"You are welcome. It was a simple stew."

"No, I do not thank you only for the food, I thank you for your excellent care of me."

She was quiet for a moment. "It is nice to have someone in the house again." He heard the door close softly behind her.

Now for more endless days of sleeping and darkness, he thought.

The Duke and Duchess of Loring had an uneventful trip across the Channel. Lord Vernon and Beatrice had joined them and planned to continue on south from the port. The Duchess was on her best behaviour thus far, presumably grateful for her maid and for travel by coach. The Duke rode alongside, preferring sitting a horse to the cramped quarters of a carriage. The Duke had seen to his duchess's every comfort, hoping to keep her in good humour when he had the easy option to do so. It was not likely to remain the case. She had not complained, which made him more pleased with her than he would admit. They travelled quickly to Paris, anxious to discover as much as possible from Wellington and his staff. He would travel on to Brussels if necessary.

They arrived at the new British Embassy, on the Rue Du Farbourg Saint-Honoré, before even stopping at their hotel.

The Duke handed his horse to a groom, and went to open the carriage that held the Duchess.

Would you prefer to go on to the hotel? I have pushed you far this day, and I would understand if you choose to do so. We may not find out any information here, but I thought it a logical place to start.

The Duchess looked weary, but she shook her head. "No, Robert, I shall come with you. I need to know as well as you."

He helped her alight from the carriage and walk into the beautiful new embassy. The marbled entrance held a grand staircase off to one side and elegantly tall, gilded doors leading to various salons. They were not kept waiting long, and were ushered into a parlour.

Wellington and his staff were thankfully still in Paris, facilitating the peace negotiations. The army continued to occupy the north and camped in Cambroi. So far, the Duke's information appeared to be current.

The Duke came into the room, followed by their nephew, Andrew Abbott, who greeted his aunt and uncle warmly.

Wellington greeted his old friend. "Loring!"

"Wellesley! May I offer....felicitations? And condolences?" Hands were shaken, and they were seated.

"Yes, my heart is broken by the terrible loss I have sustained amongst my old friends and companions, and my poor soldiers. Believe me, nothing except a battle lost can be half so melancholy as a battle won."

"Word is, we lost over twenty thousand."

"It has been a damned serious business... Blücher and I have lost thirty thousand men. It has been a damned nice thing—the nearest run thing you ever saw in your life... By God! I don't think it would have been done if I had not been there."

"Thank God that you were."

"What brings you to Paris? I am unbelievably sorry about Fairmont."

"Pardon?"

Wellington and Andrew exchanged glances.

"Do you mean to tell me that my son was killed? We came because we had no news."

The Duchess's swoon was real, and for once, her husband could not blame her. Were he of a delicate constitution, he would like nothing more than to do the same. Instead, he was forced to hide his emotion.

He called for her maid to attend her, and went over and held her in his arms.

Once she was brought to, he addressed Wellington, "I suppose you should start from the beginning."

Wellington deferred to Andrew, "Abbott, here, knows more than I. I regret I can say no more than he was the bravest, fiercest warrior to the end. I feel his loss deeply, as do his men. I will leave you to speak as a family, but if you need me I will be in the next room."

Loring nodded and, once Wellington was gone, he looked to Andrew.

Andrew was struggling to find words. He looked toward his aunt, "Shall I wait until she is comfortable? I would like her to hear as well."

"Very well. She has been anxious to know."

Once the Duchess was comfortable again, the Duke held her hand, bracing himself for the details. Andrew pulled a chair to be near them and began his account of events.

"I cannot believe you have not heard. His batman, Ajax, was to have escorted his body back to England. They should have been there weeks ago."

The Duke shook his head. "No word of Nathaniel's body, or of his batman, has reached England. I have had investigators in Brussels and Waterloo searching, but had found nothing when we left England."

"I do not understand."

"Where did you see him last?"

"At a small farmhouse about half a mile from the battlefield. He had been carried there for his wounds to be tended. His batman was with him when I left."

"The French took him for help? Why?"

"I cannot answer for certain, but he was respected. He treated them with dignity, even though they were the enemy."

"Why were you unable to remain with him?" the Duke asked.

Andrew hesitated.

"What could have persuaded you to leave Nathaniel? That is very unlike you."

"Aunt, Uncle, I had hoped you would already know of this, but I can see I will be telling you the whole. Nathaniel sent a new Will to his solicitor, though I suppose if word of his death had not reached England, there would be no reason for the solicitor to have contacted you."

"I do not understand," the Duchess said.

Andrew nodded. "Some events unfolded before the battle began. Lady Lydia Markham arrived in Brussels... with a five-year-old child."

The Duchess drew in a scandalized breath but said nothing. The Duke waited, knowing this must have something to do with Nathaniel.

"She came here looking for Nathaniel. The child is his."

"Dear God!"

The Duchess fainted again, and her head hit the back of the sofa before the Duke could catch her. Her maid rushed to attend her, and the Duke pulled Andrew across the room to hear the remainder of the story.

"I do not believe she can stand any more shocks at this moment."

Andrew nodded, "I am sorry to be the bearer of such news. It is much to take in at one time."

"Is there any doubt this child is Nathaniel's? Did he acknowledge it?"

"There can be no doubt. I have seen her. And yes, he did. In fact, he married Lady Lydia one week before the battle."

They Duke glanced hurriedly over at the Duchess. She had not heard the latest blow. He himself had to sit down in order to digest the information.

Andrew continued to enlighten him, which only made the situation worse.

"He made certain she will be known as Lady Fairmont. He had Wellington attend as a witness, and then announced their marriage at the Duchess of Richmond's ball the night we were called to arms."

The Duke dropped his head into his hands. His son knew what he was doing. He had made it so they could not deny Lady Lydia or her bastard child.

"Where has Lady Lydia gone with my supposed grandchild? I would have expected her on my doorstep the moment she arrived back in London."

"With all due respect, sir, I do think you do Lady Lydia an injustice. If you recall, Nathaniel had courted her before he was sent to the army. I think many of her subsequent actions are explained when you consider she was left with child by his departure."

"But no one took any of his amours seriously then; he was wilder than a hound on the hunt! And she said not a word to me! Not one word! Instead, she threw herself at every eligible male in town! I do not understand why she would keep this from me and not use it to her advantage somehow."

"Does that not do her credit? The part about not asking you for help? I do not know why she chose to play the role of wanton. Perhaps what she did was out of love for the child."

"It is not in keeping with what I know of her."

"I think you may find that either she is changed, or that we did not truly know her before. I spent much time with her after the battle, and confess I had misjudged her."

The Duke raised his eyebrows sceptically, but chose not to argue with his nephew. He would have to find Lydia and determine her motives.

"Where is she? Where are they?"

"Still here in France. She wanted to make a new life for them. I escorted them to Blois and saw them placed in a small cottage there with Lady Lydia's old nurse. Unfortunately, I had to return to duty."

"Can you give me their direction?"

Andrew nodded. "Shall I escort you there?"

"I do not think that will be necessary, but I want to sleep before I make any hasty decisions. I would also like directions to where you last saw Nathaniel. I will send word to my investigators. I cannot imagine Ajax and Nathaniel disappearing into thin air, but much can happen between here and England." He struggled to control himself and looked away. "I need to know I have exhausted all possibilities. I would like to see my son buried properly."

"Of course, I too would want nothing less for my cousin and one of England's greatest heroes."

The Duke gave a stiff nod and rose to go back to his duchess.

"I will send word after we reach our hotel. I think we both need a good night's rest, and you may bring your directions to me in the morning."

Andrew embraced his aunt and uncle with much-needed affection, and they departed.

~

Wellington waved his hat. Nathaniel raised his sabre to charge the enemy. He prayed for darkness soon; he had never fought any battle such as this. He was losing stamina, and his men were done for—those that were left. They could not continue like this. The entire day of charge after charge in the suffocating heat and smoke made it difficult to take a deep breath in, and when he did, it burned. The entire Union Brigade had been wiped out, and his own had suffered heavily.

He rode deeper into the smoke and suddenly felt his left hand explode. When he looked down it was gone. It was impossible to see for the thick clouds of smoke surrounding him. Searching for something to tie off the blood flow at his wrist, he yanked off his cravat and bound his left arm, growing weak as the blood seeped from his body. He saw a bright flash and felt the earth explode beneath him. He felt Salty fall from below. He began to stand, searching on the ground for his pistol and sabre. His vision was blurred and his head was pounding. Hoof beats approached from behind, but he turned too late as the French sword thrust into him. When he looked, he saw Satan smiling down at him, holding Lydia on one arm and Amelia on the other. The devil laughed demoniacally and rode away with his two loves.

"Noooooo!" Nathaniel bolted straight out of bed, drenched in his own sweat. He searched for something to bring him back to the present, but he was lost in a sea of darkness. He fought for direction, but he was having the same nightmare over and over, and he could not change the outcome. Bits and pieces of his last fight were beginning to come back to him.

He had had enough of the torture. He had lost all sense of time and had no idea how long he had been at the farmhouse. It had to have been weeks. He was trapped inside another circle of hell. His head was still bandaged so tightly he had no idea if he would be able to see or not. The doctor was most insistent that the bandage not be removed too early or it would jeopardize his chances.

He would order Ajax to help him leave as soon as the bandages came off. If he could not see by then, he would wait no more. He did not know how he would handle the eternal darkness, for now he refused to believe it was forever. Only one of his eyes had been damaged irreparably, so he would will the other one to work.

Nathaniel was finally strong enough to get up out of the bed and sit outside for a little while each day. He was desperate to leave and find his wife and daughter. They could be anywhere by now. His nightmares would not cease until he found them, he was certain. His only reservation was how Lydia would react to him being a cripple. He knew she had seen him, but not without the bandages. It was one thing to react when you first saw an injury, but it was another thing entirely to have to adjust to daily life with someone who could never be normal again. He felt selfish, but he did not care. He wanted to be with Lydia, and he hoped she would be able to overcome any disgust with his disfigured body. He *had* to be with Amelia; he had to be part of her life and watch her grow.

He knew as a future duke that people would tolerate him. He also knew from watching others that most people's reaction had to do with how the injured acted with regard to their disabilities. He refused to be shunned for doing his duty and keeping those people safe. He refused to go back to England and not do something for the other wounded veterans who were not future dukes. But first, he needed to find his wife and daughter.

"Ajax!"

"Yes, my lord?"

"When is the doctor to return?"

"This afternoon, my lord."

"Very good. Please pack our belongings. We will leave as soon as he removes my bandages."

Ajax hesitated. He was no stranger to injury himself, and he was not one to defy orders, from his master or doctor. Nathaniel knew he was placing Ajax in an untenable position, but he also knew he was strong enough to leave. He would not be deterred.

"Ajax?"

"Yes, my lord?"

"Did you understand me? Do you disagree with my choice to leave?"

"Not exactly, sir. I consider, on the one hand, it is a good sign that you are ready to leave and are becoming...mettlesome."

"But on the other hand?"

"I...I...I am not certain how it will be if you cannot see, my lord."

"I am not certain either. But I know my wife and daughter believe me to be dead, and I cannot allow them to continue with that belief. You still have had no word from my father, then?"

"Nothing at all, my lord. Lord Wellington, his staff, and those who were able to continue on, have moved to France. I have no one else to send another message with."

"Is there anyone who knows I am alive?"

"I am not certain, my lord."

"How many times must I ask you to stop *my lording* me?"

"Beg pardon, sir."

Nathaniel let out an exasperated sigh of frustration. He hated being dependent on others, helpless. "Very well then, Ajax. See to packing our belongings, then ride into Waterloo or Brussels and find transportation. As much as I would like to think I could easily sit a horse, I will not add that burden to your worries. Blind or not, we will leave today. Find out everything you can about Wellington's where-abouts. I assume he is reigning in Paris by now, but verify that. We shall start with him. I hope Major Abbott is with Lady Lydia, but he may have rejoined Wellington by now. He had better know where she is, however."

"Yes, my lord."

"Ajax!"

"Sorry, sir."

Ajax left the room and, a little while later, Nathaniel heard the door shut and a horse ridden away. Thank God Ajax had followed his orders. He could not remain here another day. Now, if that deuced doctor would just call on him, he would demand that he remove the bandages. If the doctor refused, he would do it himself and leave anyway. It was not that he wasn't grateful for his help, or the old lady's, but he did not need coddling and he was as strong as he would be for some time. There was nothing that staying here any longer would achieve.

The doctor arrived later than Nathaniel wanted. He was sitting with his trunks packed, waiting.

"Good sir, I must protest. I can certainly remove the bandages, but that does not mean you will be able to see. I cannot say if the swelling of your brain has reduced enough for this."

"I cannot wait any longer. We must proceed."

"Very well. I cannot like it, but there is little I can do to deter you, I can see."

The doctor slowly began unwrapping the bandages that had bound Nathaniel's head for several weeks. The sensation of air hitting his face and his wound was painful. He heard the old lady begin to weep quietly, and he knew he must look horrific. The sensation of light in his right eye told him that he was not completely blind, but as the last bandage was removed and he opened his left eye, he could not focus. He blinked away the darkness and looked slowly from blurry face to blurry face, familiarizing himself with his surroundings.

"You can see!"

"Yes, but my eyes cannot seem to adjust."

"That will improve. Your eye muscles have grown weak from disuse. We must fashion a cover for your other side. The wound is healing well, but it will be more comfortable if it remains covered."

"Or people who must look at me will be more comfortable." Nathaniel said what no one else would.

The old lady went off to see to creating a cover for the left side of Nathaniel's face, and the doctor proceeded to warn him about over-exerting himself.

Nathaniel thanked him kindly, but dismissed him and paid for his services. The old lady could not stop weeping and hugging him and Ajax. She had grown attached to them and had enjoyed having her home filled once again, she told them. Nathaniel paid her for her troubles, despite her protests. He sat down for her to fit the patch she had sewn for him.

"Still so handsome. She traced her fingers over the scar that trailed down his face. Your wife will not mind."

Nathaniel smiled at her kindness. He took hold of her hands and brought them up for a kiss fit for royalty. *"Merci, Madame, au revoir.* I am ever grateful for your kindness."

CHAPTER 19

It was nearing autumn, though the temperatures were so mild one would hardly have noticed. Lydia sat on the large wooden swing and rocked back and forth. It seemed swinging was an ageless pleasure. She enjoyed it as much as Amelia did. She looked out over the vineyards: it was time for harvest. Amelia was excited, for she had been promised the pleasure of stomping grapes.

Lydia could not believe it had been three months since Nathaniel had died. Amelia loved France and was adapting to the language and culture beautifully. She was doted upon by everyone on the estate. Monsieur Clement was kind to her, allowing her to run tame with his own children. She had cast her spell on them as well.

Lydia was still happy with her choice to come here, but there was something beginning to nag at the back of her mind about returning Amelia to England so she could know her paternal grandparents, even if it was only for a short visit. But would they accept her? Would they want to see her? She did not know how she would handle having her angel rejected. There was always the opposite possibility that they might want to take her away. That was something she would not allow to happen. More likely, she thought, they would be uninterested. She knew Major Abbott had sent word to his uncle, and Nathaniel had sent a copy of the Will to his solicitor. She had expected to hear something by now, even if it was an objection to their marriage.

Could she return? Her figure would appreciate it, but she was not sure if she was ready. Maybe next spring. At least she no longer cried every day. In the beginning, she would curl up in the corner and cry for no reason, or find herself staring blankly at the wall. She had been tired all day but could not sleep at night. Amelia had heard her crying and cuddled up next to her. She should have been a comfort to her daughter, but Amelia had helped her instead.

She picked up speed on the swing. It was exhilarating to feel the wind in her face. She had never been allowed to do such things as a child. She was sure it had not been considered proper, even as a child, then. If only her aunt could see her now!

"Lady Fairmont?" Lydia heard a booming voice. She knew that voice. Oh, heavens, she must look a sight. She slowed herself down and climbed from the swing.

The Duke and Duchess of Loring were standing there looking at her, the Duchess in astonishment and the Duke with something akin to amusement.

Lydia stood there dumbstruck. It was as if they had known she was thinking about them and they'd appeared. It was a moment before she could recollect herself enough to curtsy and greet her husband's parents.

"Your Graces. I am surprised to see you here."

"Probably not as surprised as we are," the Duke replied.

Lydia blushed. They were not going to make this easy, were they?

"I suppose you have heard about Lord Fairmont. I am terribly sorry for your loss."

The Duke looked away and the Duchess blotted her eyes with her handkerchief. They still stood awkwardly.

"Forgive my manners. Would you like to come inside? Have you journeyed far today?" Lydia asked, as she led them into her parlour.

"About halfway from Paris. My nephew gave us your direction. I hope you do not mind us coming without warning," asked his Grace.

"Not at all, you are most welcome." Lydia rang for tea, then directed them to sit down. "I suppose you have a lot of questions for me."

"Actually, I believe that my nephew answered most everything. However, I would like to see my grandchild."

The Duchess had remained silent, but this caused her to cry.

"What are your intentions with respect to Amelia?" Lydia tried to remain calm, but was terrified of the Duke's response.

"My nephew assures me that she is Nathaniel's daughter. I had hoped we might become acquainted."

Lydia was not surprised that they questioned Amelia's paternity. She knew her behaviour had been questionable in London. She doubted they would understand why, or even care to.

"Amelia should be back soon. She has been learning to ride with the Clement children, and taking lessons with them. Do you plan to stay long?"

"I suppose that depends. We are still searching for Nathaniel."

"I beg your pardon? I thought his batman was to return his body to England?"

"That did not happen. I have had investigators searching for him for months. Andrew told me of the farmhouse where he left him. I have sent word for the search to resume there."

"What could have happened? I suppose any number of things."

"Mama, Mama! Look what I have!" The spitting image of Nathaniel with curls ran through the front door into her mother's arms, her cat tucked under one arm.

Lydia knelt down, "What do you have, my darling?"

"Monsieur Clement made me gwape juice! That's what the gwapes turn into after you squash them before they become wine!"

"Wonderful! I will have to try some later. But first, there is someone here who would like to meet you."

Amelia turned to see the formidable-looking guests. She shied back behind her mother's skirts. It was one thing when she was comfortable enough to initiate talking to someone, Lydia knew. It was another thing entirely with strangers. Strangers who were both staring at her with wide eyes and open mouths.

"Who are they, Mama?"

"These are your grandparents, Amelia. May I introduce the Duke and Duchess of Loring. They are your papa's parents."

Amelia looked them over, and clearly decided if they were related to her papa they could not be too awful. She came out from behind Lydia's skirts and performed a beautiful curtsy. "How do you do? I am Amelia."

What happened next astonished Lydia as much as anything she had ever seen. The Duke squatted down on his heels, and the Duchess knelt beside him. He opened his arms to Amelia and she ran into them gladly.

"Oh, Robert. It is like looking at Nathaniel twenty years ago. I can hardly believe it."

"Hello, my beautiful darling."

The Duke picked Amelia up and sat on the sofa with her in his lap. *Chaton* followed. The Duchess joined them on the sofa and reached up and stroked her granddaughter's curls.

"What shall I call you?" Amelia asked looking up to her grandparent's faces.

"That is a good question. What should you like to call us?"

The little girl thought deeply and then decided, "How about gwandpapa and gwandmama?"

"I think that would be perfect. Now tell me about this grape juice."

Lydia watched the normally rigid Duchess transform before her eyes. Both the Duke and Duchess were enthralled with Amelia. Lydia should not have been surprised. She sat back and observed as her daughter captivated them with her tales of stomping grapes, riding her pony—the one her papa had given her—and her French lessons. Lydia was so proud of the child whom she and Nathaniel had made. If only he could be here to enjoy this moment.

After Nurse came to take Amelia away, Lydia asked the question she most feared.

"What happens next, sir?"

"We had planned to stay here until we have word about Nathaniel. Beatrice and Vernon have purchased a villa down the coast. We were hoping you might consider joining us there, so we may all get to know one another better."

Lydia smiled. So Beatrice had finally brought Vernon to the altar, and now they were sisters.

The Duke continued, "After that, I am not certain. We would be happy if you would return to England with us. I will not press you for an answer now."

"Thank you. I am not certain I know. I am still taking one day at a time. I would be delighted to visit Beatrice, however. I think she would be thrilled to meet her niece."

"I will make arrangements then."

"You might have to consult your granddaughter, first. I promised her she could stay for the harvest. If she is ready to go, then so am I."

This elicited a hearty chuckle from the Duke. The Duchess gave a slight smile, but was abnormally quiet.

Lydia was certain her daughter was one step away from being spoiled.

Nathaniel had misjudged his strength. He felt wretched as they rode along the rain-rutted road to Paris. He had to continue on. It had been three months since Waterloo. He was grateful, however, that he was not obliged to ride on horseback, for he would have embarrassed himself.

Ajax had been able to determine that Wellington and his staff had gone to Paris. The remainder of the British Army was in the north of France across the border. But he needed to find Andrew. If Abbott was not with Wellington, then he would at least know where he was. It took them a few days to reach Paris, despite having a carriage.

Nathaniel suffered megrims and those caused him to be sick more often than not. The doctor said it was to be expected after an injury to the head. His vision had not fully recovered either, but he would not complain. He was grateful to be alive.

Ajax helped him from the carriage when they arrived at the embassy. The butler had to visibly control himself from cringing at the sight they made. Even Nathaniel could see his reaction. No matter. He really was not bothered. They were shown into the salon, and he requested Major Abbott, if he was available.

When Andrew came into the room, Nathaniel had to laugh. He had never witnessed someone seeing a ghost before.

Andrew stood still and paled.

"Please tell me you do not intend to swoon, Andrew, however flattering it might be to think I had unmanned you so."

"How is this possible?" Andrew looked between Ajax and Nathaniel. "I…I saw you with my own eyes!"

"I suspect I appeared dead because of the large dose of laudanum the doctor gave me to ease my way into the afterlife."

"By God, you do have more lives than a cat!" Andrew shook his head and went over to hug his cousin. As he put his arms around him, he stopped himself from squeezing. "Are you fully healed?"

"Honestly? No, but well enough. Where have Lydia and Amelia gone? Back to England?"

"No. She did not wish to return. I saw them settled in a cottage along the Loire, near Orléans."

"So they are near?"

"A two-day drive."

"Is there a chance Hookey will let you escort me?"

"I do not think it will be a problem. I would be deuced grateful to leave these negotiations. These are my father's preserve, not mine."

"Let us ask him, then. Is he crusty today?"

"No more than usual. I am certain he will be happy enough to see you alive that it will not matter."

"How bad were the losses? I know it was beyond my imagination."

"We still do not have exact totals. We think it over thirty thousand Allied deaths alone."

Nathaniel let out of whistle. That was more than he had thought possible. How could one day be so horrific?

"They have still not finished burying the dead. The infirmaries are still overrun."

"I doubt I would be alive, had I ended up in one."

"It is amazing you survived your doctor!"

"He did not try to kill me again after that." He laughed. "He was convinced I survived by divine intervention and was somewhat in awe of me after that."

Wellington was not available, and Nathaniel was exhausted.

"I will see to Hookey when he has time. You get some rest."

"Much obliged."

Andrew found him a room, and they planned to set out to find Lydia the next day.

"May we leave in the morning? I have already lost so much time."

"I do not think it will be a problem. Oh! Your parents were here a week ago searching for you."

"My father did not receive my letters, then?" he asked quietly.

Andrew shook his head, "Apparently not. They went to find Lydia and to meet Amelia."

"Well, I suppose it shall be one grand reunion then. How did my parents take the news?"

"Of your death, of your marriage, or of your child?"

Nathaniel barked a sardonic laugh. "All of it, I suppose."

"My aunt swooned, of course. My uncle took it as well as could be expected."

"We had best make haste at all events. I do not want Lydia to suffer any more."

Another two miserable days in the carriage passed for Nathaniel. He normally enjoyed travel, especially when he'd had the luxury of riding his own horse, *Salty*. He hoped his beloved comrade had died a swift death. He could still hear the painful whinnying of the wounded horses on the battlefield. Salty was the reason he was still alive today. He had been through more with that beast than any human.

It might be years before he could sit a horse again, if ever. He could not waste his energy worrying about that for now. His priority was finding his wife and daughter. That is what gave him hope. He looked down at the place where his hand used to be. It still felt as if there were a hand there. It pained him horribly at times. How could something that was not there bother him? It was an enigma.

Andrew helped to distract him by telling jokes of Hookey's antics in the peace negotiations. They avoided speaking about the many friends they had lost. It was too painful, and they chose to fix their attention on the present.

"Tell me about the place you left my family. How were they getting on?"

"It is a beautiful place. I must admit Lady Fairmont has excellent taste. We happened upon it by luck. The owner of the accommodation we had in Orléans suggested the cottage. I am not certain the owner had wished to hire it out, but it is hard to resist your beautiful wife and enchantress daughter."

Nathaniel laughed. "Should I be concerned I will no longer find my wife a widow?"

"I doubt it. The *Monsieur* was certainly handsome, but Lady Fairmont's elder by at least fifteen years. She was too grieved to notice him, however."

"That is something to be grateful for, I suppose," Nathaniel said sarcastically.

However, when they finally arrived at Maison Belle Vue, they were to be disappointed.

"I am sorry, monsieur. The lady and child, they left with *le Duc* and *la Duchesse* a few days ago."

"Do you have any idea where they went?"

"I am sorry, no. I heard them speak of the coast, but that is all."

Nathaniel had to walk away and take deep breaths. He needed something, anything at this point. He needed to punch something to relieve his frustration. Or perhaps fall to his knees and cry. That might be all that was left to him as he looked at his stump.

After a few minutes, Andrew came over to him. "Do not give up yet. An entourage of a duke, with a beautiful lady and small child, would not go unnoticed. We can take the main road toward the coast and hope that they were seen."

Nathaniel sighed, then nodded. He was grateful Andrew had come along. He was too exhausted to think straight. He wanted this to be over with as soon as possible.

They found the *Monsieur*, and prepared to take their leave.

"Wait! *S'il vous plaît!*"

The men stopped and turned. The *Monsieur* smiled. "Please take some grape juice to the young lady. It was her favourite."

They were loaded up with several crates of wine and grape juice before they made their departure. Nathaniel was tempted, sorely tempted, as the pain in his head throbbed an unkind reminder of that unforgettable day.

They managed to track the Duke's entourage all the way south to Toulouse—another battle better forgotten. Nathaniel certainly never thought he would be on the old Peninsular Campaign trail again.

"Why ever were they heading in this direction?" After endless travel, Nathaniel was becoming exasperated with this chase.

"Perhaps they are joining Vernon and Beatrice."

"Pardon?"

"Vernon mentioned they were celebrating their wedding trip on the coast."

"And this just now occurred to you?"

"I am sorry. It did not seem likely that parents would be welcome on a honeymoon."

"You did not even mention they had married!"

"I did not know until I saw your parents in Paris. It must not have had time to assimilate into my conscious thought."

"Well at least we have not lost much time. Kindly direct Ajax to head east. I know where they are."

"How can you know with such certainty?"

"Our friend Vernon always had an affinity for this area when we were here before. He would prattle on and on about the warm sunny beaches and spending winters here. Unless I am mistaken, he is less than twenty miles from here, sunning his pathetic *derriere*."

"I for one will be ecstatic to see that pathetic *derriere*," Andrew retorted.

"If that pathetic *derriere* comes with my beautiful wife and daughter, so will I."

CHAPTER 20

$\mathcal{N}$athaniel wanted to see Lydia before informing everyone else that he was alive. Andrew had enquired after her before Nathaniel made his presence known. She was out for her morning constitutional. Vernon had purchased an incredible château with vast vineyards and magnificent views of the Mediterranean. It had not taken Nathaniel long to ascertain their whereabouts, once he had realized they were looking for Vernon and Beatrice.

He hoped Lydia had not walked all the way to the coast. He was not strong enough to make it that far yet, but he wanted to see her first. Andrew had told him how she had searched endlessly for him on the battlefield, and he knew that that alone must have been the worst vision she had ever seen. Then, to have seen him near death—to believe him to be dead—he could not imagine what she had been through these past months. He saw her standing in the garden, gazing out over the crystal blue waters, looking deep in thought and more handsome than ever. Though his sight was not fully restored, he could still perceive her beauty.

"Lydia."

She turned and fainted dead away when she saw him. He should have predicted that would happen. He went over to her and knelt down to try to rouse her awake by stroking her cheek.

She began to stir. "Leave me alone," she grumbled.

"Lydia. Lydia!" He shook her a little, growing concerned she might have hit her head.

She shook her head back and forth, with her eyes still closed. "Leave me, I beg. I was having a dream that Nathaniel was here and I don't want it to end."

He smiled. Having a dream, was she? Perhaps he could make it better. He bent over and began to kiss her in a way that she would never forget.

When he finally came up for a breath, he felt a hard slap on the face.

"What was that for? I thought it rather a nice gesture," he said as he rubbed his face. That was going to leave a mark.

"I had to make sure it wasn't another dream."

"Are you convinced?"

"You had better kiss me again to make sure." She lay there, smiling dreamily. He laughed.

"Perhaps we should move somewhere other than the garden." They had better do so, or he might lose control. More than six years was a long time to wait.

"The garden is fitting for a dream."

"But not for five-year-old eyes," Nathaniel said dryly.

Her eyes popped open. "No, not for a five-year-old's eyes. Has she seen you yet?"

"No. I found you first." He smiled.

"No one else knows?"

"Andrew might have told them by now. He gave me a few minutes' grace."

"Remind me to thank him later." She traced the scar along his cheek, from the patch covering his eye downward.

He shivered. He would probably never get used to the feel of someone touching his scars, but he would tolerate anything she did. He knew she needed time to adjust to him as well.

"Does that bother you?" Lydia asked worriedly.

"It is an unusual sensation. Does it disgust you? You need not feel obligated to perform your marital duties. However, you will never be able to get rid of me again."

"If you think that scar makes you less handsome, then you are sadly mistaken."

"And my hand? Or lack, thereof?"

"Mm-mm." She shook her head. "I never understood why people were bothered by such things. You fought valiantly for our country. It is a badge of honour." She swallowed. "If others only knew what it was like…"

"Most could not be so inconvenienced. I am glad that you feel that way, however." He smiled, and began to lean over to kiss her again.

"Papa! Papa!"

Amelia ran over and practically attacked them. She wrapped her arms around Nathaniel and squeezed tight. He had to ignore the pain in his side, but there was never anything more worth it.

"I knew you would come back! Does this mean we are in heaven now? Did you bring angels with you, Papa?" she asked with exuberance.

"We are not in heaven, my darling, but this is a very close second."

"I never thought you were dead, Papa. I knew you would find me. What happened to youw face and youw hand? You look like a piwate!" She touched all of his visible wounds with curiosity.

"I only lack a hook for a hand and a wooden leg," he said with amusement.

"I think I pwefer you like this. You could not wide with me if you had a wooden leg. And a hook might accidetawy hurt the horse," Amelia said with a frown.

"Very true. I suppose I will have to forgo the hook." He reached up and smoothed out her frown.

"You can keep the patch. I like that," she said as she continued to examine him.

"As you wish, sweetheart. Do you think we could get off the

ground, now? I should probably go and re-introduce myself to the rest of the family."

"Uncle Andwew alweady told everybody. They are waving smelly bottles under Grandmama's nose."

Nathaniel and Lydia laughed.

The reunited family made their way back to the house. Nathaniel felt as if he was the luckiest man alive. He had been given another chance. He had Lydia's arm tucked into his and Amelia on his other arm. He did not ever want to let them go again.

"Well, well, well. Is this not a charming scene?" a sinister voice spoke from behind them.

"Uncle," Lydia gasped and spun around. "What are you doing here?"

"What do you think I am doing?"

"I cannot imagine what business you would have in southern France." Her uncle had a look in his eye she had seen before, but now it held madness.

"Can you not?" he said menacingly. "Do you know how long it has taken to track you down?"

"Amelia, go back to the house and tell Nurse it's time for tea. We will join you shortly." Lydia attempted to project a calm she did not feel. Amelia glanced at the visitor sceptically, but climbed down from her papa and ran to the house.

"Fairmont, do you know what your *lovely Lydia* has been doing in your absence? Not pining for you, but whoring herself to me."

This was met with silence and an icy glare.

Lydia had hinted to Nathaniel of her uncle's abuse, but had not fully expounded upon her shame. She stood still, her arms wrapped around herself, biting her lip while willing her warm tears to dry. She should have known happiness was but an elusive myth not meant for the likes of her.

"You thought you could chase your old lover down and convince him to take you back? You thought to pawn your base-born brat off upon him?" Her uncle's chest was heaving, his face was flushed and a vein beat a threatening pulse in his neck. Nothing good could happen. When Nathaniel did not answer quickly, her uncle continued his tirade, presumably expecting Nathaniel to discard her. "You will pack up your things and return with me at once. We had an agreement."

"You will never touch me again," Lydia said, backing away from him.

"You will fulfil our agreement, or I will ruin you," he fumed.

"You will do no such thing to my wife," Nathaniel said with deadly quiet, stepping in front of Lydia.

"Your wife?" That was obviously not the answer he had anticipated.

"I accept full responsibility for Lydia's circumstances. It appears to me that the abuse that Lydia suffered at her guardian's hand would only harm yourself, Dannon. When you consider that the Duke and I have several other charges to lay against you, I rather think you should be more concerned for your own welfare than her reputation."

"That's preposterous," her uncle seethed. "You can prove nothing against me. I could present her bastard child as evidence."

"That is my granddaughter you speak of." The Duke's voice boomed scathingly from the terrace.

Dannon paled. Evidently he had not realized the Duke was also in residence.

"If I hear one word against my new daughter or granddaughter, I shall see to it you never set foot in London again. Is that understood?"

Dannon only glared at the Duke.

"In fact, if I have to look at your face for another moment, I may have to consider whether I will allow you to remain in England. I might have to call you out and settle this at once."

"Lydia and I had an agreement," he spat out. "But very well, let us settle this at once."

"No, Father. He is not worthy of a gentleman's honour." Nathaniel knocked him down with palpable relish.

"Castration is not good enough for him," Lydia said to the Duke.

Dannon began to stir and Nathaniel hit him again as soon as he was on his feet.

"That was much less than I longed to do, but he will never hurt you or Amelia ever again," Nathaniel said, wiping the blood from his hand and walking over to Lydia, who was considerably frightened.

"Come." Nathaniel wrapped his arm around her and began to lead her back to the house.

"I will see to it that he never bothers you again," the Duke said, standing over Dannon's prone body.

Lydia looked at the Duke gratefully. When they were up on the terrace she whispered, "I am sorry."

Nathaniel stopped and looked down at her with sorrow.

"Shh. No apologies. I do not question what you had to do in my absence. I am responsible for what happened to you." He paused to control his emotion as a tear escaped his eye. "I am grateful for another chance to make things right."

When they entered the parlour, his mother stared. Apparently the Duchess had been well prepared by Andrew for the shock. She had been crying, but she managed to stay upright.

"Mother."

She had never been as affectionate as the Duke, but she rose and embraced him. When she pulled back she looked him over, studying each of his injuries. He watched her face and saw that she had changed much. Whether from his resurrection, Beatrice's experience and subsequent marriage, or having a new grandchild, he could not say. He hoped the change was for the better. He wanted nothing more than to have his parents be a part of their lives, but he would not have Amelia brought up like Beatrice had been.

He greeted his father with a hug when he returned from disposing of Dannon. There was little to say, or that he wished to say, about what had happened during the last months. He did not wish to dwell on the past when he had been given a new life.

"What are your wishes now, my son? Would you like to return to England?"

"Not yet, Father. I do have plans for the future, but for the present, I would like to make up for lost time with my family. We need to get to know each other." He smiled at Lydia and then at his daughter, who was dangling yarn in front of a playful cat. He had dreamt of this moment for months. It was what he had survived for.

"Very well. Do, kindly, remember we also want to know your family more. I have enjoyed this past week more than I can remember." He chuckled. "Your daughter is in a fair way to being a better horseman than you ever dreamt of being."

"Of course she is. She takes after her mother," he said proudly.

"Certainly not her aunt," Beatrice said playfully, as she and Vernon came into the room. She greeted her brother warmly. "Why does everyone not simply stay here through the holidays? Then you can see how you feel, with no need to rush away. There is plenty of room here, and you would not have to see another person unless it was your desire to do so." She looked toward Nathaniel. "You may recover here in the bright sunshine." She looked back at her parents. "And you may spend as much time with Amelia as you please."

"The sunshine is lovely," Nathaniel agreed.

"Not so condemning of my affinity for southern France now, are you, Fairmont?" Vernon chided.

"I have never had a need to convalesce before," Nathaniel retorted dryly.

"Are you certain we would not be an imposition?" Lydia asked, much inclined to accept.

"More than certain." Beatrice nodded to Vernon, who nodded his agreement in return. "In fact, we would not mind if you stayed longer than the holidays, for we do not plan on returning to England until after Amelia's cousin makes his début."

The news dawned on everyone in the room at different moments, but Lydia immediately ran over to embrace her friend. "Congratulations! I suspected as much."

"Well, I say." The Duchess, who had only just become comfortable in her new status as a grandmother, was at a loss for words.

The Duke beamed with pride. "I think staying here an excellent idea. Nathaniel and Lydia also have some work to do on my heir, so I will see that Amelia does not lack for entertainment." He smiled and winked at Lydia.

Nathaniel only laughed.

Lydia was exhausted. It was the best, most tiring day she could remember. She had gone from melancholy to elation in twelve hours. Now they were alone, and she hated that she was uncertain. She did not know if he wanted her in that way or not. His kisses said he did, but their wedding night still lingered, causing her doubts. Was he healed enough, anyway?

"Nathaniel?"

He looked up from struggling with his boots.

"Shall I find Ajax to help you?"

"That is not necessary, if you would not mind doing the honours. He has had a rough go of it dealing with me and I would like him to have his own holiday."

She began to help him, but was surprised what he could do for himself with one hand. She felt his piercing grey eyes studying her. "Was there something you wished to ask me?"

Now she was nervous. Before she had touched him to help him, she had worked up the courage. She stopped and stared at her hands.

"Are you nervous to see me?" he asked, concern on his face.

"No. I wanted to ask why you did not...want to be... intimate on our wedding night." She blushed. Why was it so much harder to say it out loud?

"Did you think that I did not want you?"

She looked away. She had thought that was perhaps the case.

"The devil!" He ran his fingers through his hair. "Lydia, I did not wish to take the chance of leaving you with another child, on your own. Do you know how hard it was to hold you in my arms and not touch you?"

She shook her head and a tear rolled down her cheek.

"Come here, you silly woman," he said as he wrapped his arms around her.

"My only regret, my love, is that the experience will never be the same for you. I cannot bring back what was taken, but I hope my love will be more complete now. I have had months to regret that night."

"I am sorry that you regretted it. At the time I thought it the loveliest gesture. But after you were gone, I began to doubt. The imagination twists and turns our insecurities into horrible monsters."

"That it does. For now, I fully intend to erase all of your doubts and slay all of the horrible monsters."

And he did, in a very desirable fashion.

EPILOGUE

$\mathcal{H}$ad it already been two years? Nathaniel looked down at his chubby son as they celebrated his birthday. The eighteenth of June. He could not think of that day without tears coming to his eyes. He looked around at the second—no third—chance that he had been given and could still not believe any of it was real.

His son and Easton's triplets chased after the dog. His daughter and his niece laughed as they blew dandelion seeds as far as they could. He must remember to increase the gardener's wages. He sighed, but the miracles did not end there. His wife and his sister sat on a blanket under a large oak, chatting with Elinor. If anyone told him this happy family gathering would have taken place three years ago, he would have likely spat in their face for mocking him.

It had not been an easy road. He and Lydia both suffered nightmares from Waterloo. Learning to adapt to his injuries had not been pleasant either. It had made both of them determined to do something about those who were not so fortunate when they returned from war.

They had revisited the battlefield on their way back from France. He had looked over the vast field in silent reverence. It was now grown over again, benign and...peaceful. A far cry from the thousands and thousands of mangled dead and wounded they had left behind on that dreadful day. But it had helped provide some closure, knowing that it had ended, that the ground no longer cried out with the songs of mourning and sorrow; that the valley no longer echoed with cannon shot, or pistol fire, or cries of anguish.

They were able to retrieve some soldiers from the infirmaries and bring home those who had nothing left to return to, who could no longer face reality, or were unwanted.

He looked up at the home for veterans they had opened and felt a sense of pride. His father had set the building in motion at his request when he and the Duchess had returned to England. It sat near the school Easton and Elinor had built—a place where all were respected, wanted, and loved, if they could accept it.

Nathaniel, Easton and Vernon were proposing the reforms they wanted in Parliament, and all of their friends and former soldiers employed everyone possible on their various estates. Those that were unemployable lived at the home where they received care from Dr. McGinnis and his pupils from Easton and Elinor's school. They were still attempting to lure Dr. Craig away from Scotland to join them.

"Papa! Papa!"

"Uncle Andrew needs your help!" Amelia pointed to where his cousin lay on the ground.

Nathaniel looked up from wool-gathering to see Andrew being tackled by five toddlers and a feline admirer. He laughed as he watched his cousin attempt to extricate himself from the tangle, but even with a toddler on each limb and a cat rubbing on his ankles, he was still outnumbered. They were searching through his pockets in an attempt to find something. Andrew started to put one atop his head when the fathers had mercy on him and retrieved their offspring.

"What on earth possessed you to say the word *bon-bons* around a flock of children?" Nathaniel chastised playfully.

"I was trying to bribe them, of course. Besides, I rather expected they knew it was impolite to beg. Or attack." He scooped up *Chaton*, to her delight, and rubbed behind her ears, eliciting loud purrs.

Nathaniel scoffed loudly. "Little you know, then."

"How *would* I know? I haven't set up my nursery. I do not even have a wife!"

"That should be remedied," a female voice said knowingly.

"Yes, indeed. You are not getting any younger, Andrew," his sister's voice agreed.

"We would be glad to help," a third female said, trying not to laugh.

Andrew spun around and attempted to glare at his sister, cousin and friend. "Who speweth such venom yet dare not speaketh to my face?"

They all laughed to his face.

"Were you not hanging on the sleeves of the Ashbury triplets? Whatever became of them?" Beatrice asked.

"I do not hang on sleeves, Bea." He did his best dignified look, or so it appeared to Nathaniel, watching with relish.

"It did seem as though you were always dancing with them," Elinor added.

"There were three, so naturally it looked as though I were always with one of them," he said defensively.

"I do not believe they ever returned from France after Waterloo," Lydia said.

They all remained silent, a natural occurrence for any mention of that reverent place. Over, but not forgotten. Not here, at any rate.

Amelia ran over, interrupting their thoughts.

"Will you play a game with us, Papa?" she pleaded with her big grey eyes.

"Beware, Nate, that is what got me into trouble," Andrew warned.

"Ah, but I have more practice at this," he smiled haughtily.

"Yes, Andrew, it is an art." Easton laughed.

"Please share the details with me then. Olivia has me wrapped around her finger and she knows it already," Vernon self-admonished with an unrepentant smile.

"I'm going to be sick. Besides, you are practised with your own children. I suffered an allied affront by all of them at once," Andrew countered.

The children grew impatient and began to tug on their fathers' coats.

"What do you wish to play, my darling?" Nathaniel asked his eldest.

"Pall mall!" she said excitedly.

"I'm not sure the little ones can hold up the mallets." Nathaniel answered.

"Must they play?" she asked in frustration.

Nathaniel simply gave his daughter a look. "May we shoot arrows?"

"No."

"Go fishing?"

She received a head shake. She wrinkled up her face in frustration.

"There is nothing they can do but roll a ball and drool, Papa."

The men had to laugh. They could empathize with her completely.

"Would you like me to join you for a ride, Amelia?" put in Andrew. "I would not mind spending time with my god-daughter. If that is acceptable to your parents, of course."

"Traitor," the other fathers said in unison.

"You are experts at children. I am not. When they can carry on a conversation you may send them my way."

"Oh, thank you, Uncle Andrew!" She threw her arms around him gratefully. "I will go and change my dress." She ran off to don her riding habit. The men looked after her with long faces.

"When did she lose the Andwew?" Andrew asked sadly.

"She is very proud that she has learned to say her Rs properly," Nathaniel replied.

"I do not care for it, personally."

"They grow up quickly."

Elinor came over, "Pardon my interruption. Easton, would you mind helping me allow the children to splash about in the water since it is such a warm day?"

"That sounds like a famous idea! I will join you," Vernon offered.

"And I," Beatrice spoke. "You will need all available hands."

Nathaniel and Lydia watched the scene from the banks. He was comfortable with his injuries, but he did not expose them more than necessary.

"Can you believe this is our life, now?"

He shook his head. "No." Never a day went by that he did not wake up knowing how fortunate he was.

"What are you thinking about?"

"How fortunate I am."

"We both are."

"Yes." He reached around her from behind and placed his hands on her growing belly and perched his head on her shoulder. "I had always thought redemption would mean forgetting my transgressions."

"To quoth the wise bard: *What's done cannot be undone.*"

"Aye. I now believe it means remembrance and forgiveness."

"And love." She turned her head for a meaningful kiss.

"Never forget love."

AUTHOR'S NOTE

Many of us die-hard Regency fans have read and re-read Georgette Heyer's books, *An Infamous Army* and *Spanish Bride*. I credit her with sparking my interest in the impact that warring with Napoleon had on the era. I was privileged to live near to Waterloo for a time, and fell in love with the people and the culture. I could do without their malodorous fertilizing, however! That was very real, and a frequent topic of conversation amongst us foreigners living there. The hardest part for me was to tell a story in the same environment as her books and not seem like I was copying her work. She was incredibly detailed in her research and I found no matter where I looked, she had taken much of her dialogue and scenes from Wellington and many of the notable characters themselves. So please allow me the liberties I have taken. I have only included what I thought necessary for historical accuracy. And to the real commander of the 1st Life Guards, Lt Col Samuel Ferrier, I humbly beg your pardon and hope I represented your position well.

The other part I found difficult was trying to tell a story from a rapist's eyes. It is never excusable, and I hope I portrayed that he knew he was responsible for his actions. I tried to put myself in the shoes of someone who had done something unforgivable and try to put the pieces of their life back together again. A few tears *might* have been shed in the writing of this book.

PREVIEW SHADOWS OF DOUBT

*G*wendolyn wanted to get away from Bath. She had lived here her whole life and wanted to see the rest of the world. Desperately. She knew there was more to life, because she had read such things in books. But as long as her mother was ill, and she had no money, she would have to be content with travelling through the written word. She fastened her bonnet and prepared to take advantage of this small reprieve. One of her mother's cousins and childhood playmates had moved to Bath and had been coming to visit for a few hours each day to sit with Mama, allowing Gwendolyn to have some fresh air. She pulled her bonnet down over her unruly mane, and set out for her walk.

Mama got anxious when she was alone. She had a servant in the house with her, but that was not the same. Thank goodness Mama was happy with her cousin. The time Gwendolyn had each day was a treasure. How had she maintained her sanity before?

She wandered around on the beautiful sunny day with little purpose, enjoying the taste of freedom. She walked down Milsom Street on her way to the circulating library and passed the colour-man's shop. She wished she could still afford to buy paints, brushes and canvas. *Keep walking*, she told herself. There was no point in letting her artist's genie out of the bottle, since she could not indulge it. She normally walked in a different direction so she would not allow herself to be tempted by things she could never have again. The dress shop next door had a celestial blue silk hanging in the window that she felt a pang of envy for.

She had long ago given up on having a London Season, or even one in Bath. She might have had a right to be there by her birth, but that was where the connection ended. The two times she had been to the assembly, she had lurked in the shadows because she was insecure. She was never completely comfortable in large crowds—people tended to stare. She had also been forced to leave her school when her papa died. She knew most things properly, but had had little actual practice.

Still, it would have been nice to dress up like a princess and dance with a handsome prince. Once.

She had given up on those dreams. Since Papa had died, leaving them penniless, and Mama needed her, any thoughts of her own situation were fruitless. She had missed the desirable age for marriage, and who would want to saddle themselves with an old, penniless spinster and her ailing mother? She did not want to ponder how she would manage when her mama passed away.

She scanned the available works, all familiar and most nearly memorized. Burney, Edgeworth…

She heard the clock chime. Was it so late already? She would be obliged to run if she did not leave soon. She carefully selected her two allotted volumes. Even though the cost of a library subscription was dear, she had nothing else she would rather spend her money on. It was her escape from reality;, her dreams fulfilled in another world.

She entered their rooms on Barnett Street breathlessly and tossed her bonnet on the table. She hoped she had returned before the Dowager left.

"Gwen, is that you?" she heard her mother's voice say quietly.

"Yes, Mama. Shall I bring in tea?"

"Not yet. Come in."

That was strange. Gwen walked into the parlour, a concerned look shaping her face. She curtsied to the Dowager and rushed over to her mother's side. She did not look well.

"Is something amiss?" she asked worriedly.

"No, my love. Cousin Henrietta has an invitation for you."

"Yes, your mother and I were discussing what is to be done with you. We have decided that you should accompany me to the assembly tonight," the Dowager Duchess of Loring pronounced.

"That is extremely kind of you, your Grace, but I could not." Gwen made meaningful eyes toward her invalid mother on the sofa. How could she think she could leave her?

"Your mother will be quite well. We will only be a stone's throw away. I will send an extra servant here, who may fetch you should your mother need you. She will not be alone."

Gwen did not want to go. She was past the point of being marriageable and she was certainly too poor to attract any notice. If only she had had such an offer before her world had come crashing down. She felt a twinge of guilt. She should not have been dreaming earlier...

"As grateful as I am for your offer, your Grace, I no longer own anything suitable for an assembly. Perhaps another time." She smiled gratefully. There would never be another time and she knew it.

Her mother lifted her head off her pillow and looked directly at her. "Gwendolyn, I want you to go. I need you to go, for me."

She suffered momentary astonishment. Was this her mother speaking? Her mother fretted if she left the room for more than ten minutes. She looked back at the Dowager, who nodded at her.

"Very well, Mother. If that is your wish."

The Dowager stood up. "I must take my leave, Millicent. Gwendolyn, would you be so kind as to see me to the door?"

"Of course, your Grace."

"I will send my maid over to help you dress. The carriage will come for you at seven." She leaned closer and said quietly, "Your mother is worried about what will become of you. Oblige her by appearing to enjoy yourself." She smiled knowingly at her and walked out of the door.

~

He was being set up. And the worst part was, he knew it and his grandmother knew it, and she knew that he knew that she knew he knew. But he had already agreed to attend beforehand, so he was committed and she knew it. He did not mind meeting new people--a distant relation even--and he certainly did not mind helping out, especially someone who was in need, as his grandmother had so painstakingly put it. However, he knew her motives were deeper than that. She had a look in her eye, a certain twinkle, as when she was on a mission.

He had made a point of avoiding being the object of one of her missions—until now. Unfortunately, he was the last man standing.

"Very well, Gran. Tell me. Is she four-score with warts, or is she sixteen with spots and eight chins?"

"Andrew Charles Abbott!"

He refused to feel guilty. He crossed his arms and stared.

His grandmother was nearly an octogenarian, and she had not reached that age without acquiring some skills.

"What is it you want from me? To smile at her? To dance with her twice? To bring her lemonade?"

"That all sounds lovely, yes." His grandmother nodded her satisfaction.

"And?" he prompted.

"That is all. Nothing more." She was silent, obviously trying to look innocent.

"And?" He stopped his pacing and stared.

"Well, perhaps..."

"Aha! I knew it!"

"Young man, you forget yourself. You interrupted your grandmother. Now, sit down. You are irritating my delicate constitution."

He snorted. "As delicate as a..."

"Enough. I do not need any vulgar analogies. I was going to say some conversation would be nice. I know better than to attempt to force you in to anything."

He looked at her sceptically.

"Besides, she is a highly ineligible match: a penniless spinster. She missed her début when her father died in debt, and has spent her bloom caring for her invalid mother, my cousin Millicent. I agreed to look after her if something should happen, to help her find an eligible position. She has little hope for anything more."

Andrew let out a whistle. His grandmother was serious. Now he pitied the poor girl. "I beg your pardon. I assumed you already had the wedding arranged in your mind."

"I?" She looked offended.

He knew it to be an act.

"Very well. I will try to show her a nice evening. If she is capable." Some ladies were not.

"That's my boy. I knew you would understand."

He reached over and kissed her on the cheek. She patted his cheek in return. He was sure he was being manipulated somehow, but he just didn't know what he could do about it.

Hanson arrived and had trouble disguising her shock when she saw Gwen. Wild would not be the exact word Gwen would use to describe her hair, but when she considered the shade of red and the long curls that escaped her every effort to contain them, she supposed the description apt. She should be used to the stares after six-and-twenty years.

"Hello, Hanson. I see her Grace did not warn you how much work I would be. You need not bother with my hair. It is impossible. No one has ever been able to tame it."

Hanson smiled and removed her mob cap.

Gwen burst out laughing. "I see you understand."

"Yes, miss. I can manage the hair. First, let us try the gown on. Mary, here, will make any alterations necessary, while I style your locks."

"Did you say gown?" Gwen turned to see another maid holding a fabric-wrapped gown and held it up when Hanson indicated. The two worked to unfurl the dress and hang it up for her to view.

She had no words. She looked at her old faded gown that she had planned to wear, six years out of fashion at least, and could not find words.

"It is one of her Grace's granddaughter's, that she left here. Her colouring and size are similar. It should do nicely." Hanson knew her thoughts. It was as magnificent as the silk she had seen that day in Milsom Street.

Gwen stood in disbelief as the maids helped her into the gown and pinned the necessary adjustments for her frame. She almost looked beautiful again. She should pinch herself and wake up.

"This is a mistake." She shook her head back and forth.

"Pardon, miss?"

"I cannot go. There is no point. Why pretend?"

"Miss, you'll pardon my saying so, but what's the harm?"

"A taste of something I will never have again is the harm."

"I see ye like books." The maid indicated the ones Gwen had just brought from the library.

Gwen nodded, wondering what Hanson was alluding to.

"Pretend yer the heroine of a book. Dance with yer handsome prince."

"As if one would dance with me." She shook her head. "I am sorry. Self-pity is unbecoming at best."

She saw the maid's point, but this was different. There would be real people with whom she would have to engage, people who were not comfortable socially with someone who had lost everything. The poor widow and spinster daughter. And her looks. If she was rich and titled, people would call her exotic.

"Her Grace thought ye might try to change her mind and said to remind ye of yer mother."

Gwen sighed. Her mama had been adamant, which was strange.

"Oh, very well." It might be her last chance.

She stepped out of the gown, and Mary went to work on it.

"Now for your hair." Gwen tried not to get her hopes up. She had never had her own maid to dress her hair. She had not had her locks cut in years. She unwound the untidy knot and her hair fell down her back in riots of curls.

She expected the silence. Hanson finally broke it.

"Mary, if you would please fetch me some scissors and pomade. And oil."

"Oil?" Gwen questioned in fear.

"Aye, miss. We are going to need everything we can find."

One hour, two feet cut off, and a bottle of hair oil later, Hanson let out a gasp of pleasure at her handiwork.

"Oh, miss! Do you have a glass you can look in?"

"My mother has a small one in her dresser."

"We have no time for that, miss," Mary reminded. "The carriage will be here to pick you up soon."

The maids helped her into the gown, and she hurried downstairs to meet the carriage.

She stopped to see how her mother did.

"Oh, Gwen!" Her mother burst into tears. Well, going to the assembly had been a nice thought. She should have known her mother could never go through with it.

"It is all right, Mother," she said in resignation. She bent over to comfort her. "I will not leave you." She resigned herself to staying at home after all and began to sit down.

"No! You will wrinkle your gown. I am only crying because of how beautiful you look. I have taken your life away from you."

"No, Mama. Father did that."

Through her mother's weeping she did not hear the carriage roll up.

"I beg your pardon, miss," Hanson spoke up. "The carriage is here to fetch you."

"Go! Do not worry about me."

She looked at her weak and weeping mother hesitantly but nodded, kissed her on the cheek, and went to the door.

She nearly fell as the door opened upon her.

"Oh!"

Two large hands steadied her.

A deep voice said, "I beg your pardon, miss."

She looked upward into a set of stunning blue eyes. She was speechless.

Apparently, so was he.

She heard the sound of a throat being cleared from the carriage.

"Miss Lambert, this is my grandson, Major Andrew Abbott."

This was the poor, old, penniless spinster? His grandmother must have been playing a joke on him. He snapped his jaw shut. He hadn't realized he had left it gaping open. He would play along for tonight. He escorted her to the carriage. He sat across from the girl and tried not to stare. He had never seen anything like her. She did not look old or penniless. He braved a sideways glance at his grandmother and saw a satisfied smile spread across her face. He would really like to stick his tongue out and make a face at her. Yes, he felt like a greenhorn youth sitting across from this vision in the carriage.

"I like what Hanson did with your hair, Gwendolyn."

"Thank you, your Grace."

"Do not address me as your Grace, Gwendolyn."

"I forget."

Gwendolyn. That was a fitting name. She was blushing. Then she smiled. She had dimples. He had a weakness for dimples. And red hair. This was going to be a long night.

BIBLIOGRAPHY

Britishbattles.com

   Britishempire.co.uk

   Napoleon-series.org

   Napolun.com

   Peninsularwar.org

   Regencyredingote.wordpress.com

   Twcenter.net

   Twonerdyhistorygirls.blogspot.com

   Dowager Lady De Ros, Georgiana "Personal Recollections of the Duke of Wellington" *Murray's Magazine*, Part I, 1889.

   Duke of Wellington Arthur Wellsley, *Maxims and Opinions of Field-Marshal His Grace the Duke of Wellington, Selected From His Writings and Speeches During a Public Like of More Than Half a Century.*

AFTERWORD

Author's note: British spellings and grammar have been used in an effort to reflect what would have been done in the time period in which the novels are set. While I realize all words may not be exact, I hope you can appreciate the differences and effort made to be historically accurate while attempting to retain readability for the modern audience.

Thank you for reading *Seeking Redemption*! I hope you enjoyed it. If you did, please help other readers find this book:

1. This ebook is lendable, so send it to a friend who you think might like it so they can discover me, too.
2. Help other people find this book by writing a review.
3. Sign up for my new releases at www.Elizabethjohnsauthor.com, so you can find out about the next book as soon as it's available.
4. Come like my Facebook page www.facebook.com/Elizabethjohnsauthor or follow on Twitter @Ejohnsauthor or feel free to write me at elizabethjohnsauthor@gmail.com

ACKNOWLEDGMENTS

Many thanks to:

Jill-I wish you had not experienced grief, but thank you for the willingness to help me through this.

Peter King and Alan Henshall from the Royal Dragoons Museum. I am ever so grateful for their help with questions about Regiments, uniforms, and commissions. If there are any errors, they are fully mine!

Tessa-you are such a delight to work with!

Wilette. There are only so many ways to say thank you, but you are always there with help, guidance, and your artistic abilities.

Staci, Judy, Shae, Molly, Beth, and Tina. For being eager to help and investing in my stories.

Michelle-for all things French!

To the internet. It makes you realize how incredible historical fiction writers were who did not have the luxury of research from home.

My family, for their continuous support and encouragement. It takes a village to publish a book!

ALSO BY ELIZABETH JOHNS

Surrender the Past

Seasons of Change

Seeking Redemption

Shadows of Doubt

Second Dance

Through the Fire

Melting the Ice

With the Wind

Out of the Darkness

After the Rain

Ray of Light

First Impressions